Off on the wrong foot

It didn't take Frances long to get dressed. She sat on the bench and waited while Polly threw her leotard into her backpack and pulled her dress over her head.

"So," Frances said as they headed out into the twilight where Mrs. McAllister was waiting to drive them home, "our first ballet lesson."

"Yeah, there was only one thing wrong with it."

"What's that?" Frances asked.

"It wasn't our last."

Frances dances

by
ILENE COOPER
Illustrated by Vilma Ortiz

BULLSEYE BOOKS • ALFRED A. KNOPF

NEW YORK

For Dana Resnick

Library of Congress Cataloging-in-Publication Data
Cooper, Ilene.
Frances dances / by Ilene Cooper.
p.   cm.—(Frances in the fourth grade)
Summary: As she takes ballet lessons and participates in a school
play, a timid fourth grader confronts her fears and learns a lesson
about friendship.
ISBN: 0-679-81111-7 (pbk.) ISBN 0-679-91111-1 (lib. bdg.)
[1. Friendship—Fiction. 2. Fear—Fiction. 3. Ballet dancing—
Fiction.] I. Title. II. Series: Cooper, Ilene. Frances in the fourth grade.
PZ7.C7856Fo   1991   [Fic]—dc20   90-49469
RL: 4.5
First Bullseye Books edition: July 1991

Manufactured in the United States of America
10 9 8 7 6 5 4 3 2 1

1

frances McAllister couldn't believe her eyes. She read the sign that hung in the storefront window one more time. MISS LETICIA'S SCHOOL OF THE DANCE. Frances's heart started beating a little faster. A dancing school in Lake Lister. That was something she'd always dreamed about.

Peering through the plate glass, Frances saw workmen putting up wooden bars around the room. Great, she thought. Miss Leticia must be teaching ballet. Ever since she had seen *Swan Lake* with her parents in Milwaukee last spring, Frances had wanted to be a ballerina. She wanted to wear a stiff little tutu and pink satin ballet slippers. She wanted to twirl around the stage, gracefully moving in time to the music. Wrapping her arms around herself to keep warm in the November wind, Frances lost herself to a daydream where she was taking bows before a cheering throng.

"Hey, short stuff, how come you're just standing there hugging yourself?"

Frances blinked. There was no wildly applauding audience. Only Albert Bell, the biggest tease in the fourth grade, standing there with a stupid grin on his face.

"Oh, go away," Frances mumbled. She didn't want to get in a conversation with Albert. It would only end with her looking dumb.

But Albert must have thought she already looked dumb. "I guess you have to hug yourself. Nobody else will." He gave a laugh that sounded like a mule braying.

Frances was shy, but she was learning to talk back to Albert. "Nobody would hug you either, carrot head," she replied with a significant look at his red hair.

Albert just laughed. "Planning on taking ballet lessons?" He made it sound like "belly lessons."

"What's it to you?"

"My aunt is Miss Leticia."

"You're kidding!"

"I am not," Albert said indignantly. "She used to teach in Green Bay, but she decided to move here to be closer to her family. Like me."

Frances thought having Albert in Lake Lister was a good argument for staying in Green Bay.

"She's going to teach ballet, tap, and modern, whatever that is," Albert informed her.

"Well, maybe I'll take lessons," Frances said airily.

"You'll have to be careful. You're so short, you don't want anybody stepping on you while they twirl around."

"Good-bye, Albert," Frances said, trying to maintain her dignity as she turned to cross Main Street.

"So long, twinkle toes." His mule laugh followed her across the street as she headed toward her father's hardware store.

Lake Lister, Wisconsin, was a small town. The lake attracted tourists in the summer and during the autumn when the leaves were turning, but now when it was gray and raw, the only people walking down Main Street were the locals.

Frances didn't care. She liked Lake Lister and thought it was cozy. She was almost glad when the tourists went home and gave the town back to the people who really cared about it.

She did wish there were a few more stores open along Main Street, however. Most antique shops closed after Halloween, as did the souvenir stores. There was a variety store that was pretty good, but Crawford's, the department store, had merchandise that could only be described as boring. You had to drive out to the mall to get anything really cool. Still, there was a book shop and the Sweet Shoppe, where they had really great hamburgers and shakes, a couple of restaurants, and the drugstore. McAllister's Hardware, her father's store, stayed open all year long, too.

The doorbell tinkled as Frances walked into the store. The first person she saw was her brother Mike carrying a big cardboard box over to the plumbing section. He helped out after school and on Saturdays.

"Where's Dad?" she asked, walking over to him.

"Helping someone find the right screw."

Mike let out a small groan as he put down the heavy box marked SNAKES.

Frances uttered a small scream as she glanced at the box. "Snakes?" she asked with a quaver in her voice.

Mike shook his head and adopted the disgusted tone he'd been using since he'd started high school in the fall. "Snakes to clear out a drain, dopey."

Sometimes Mike was as hard to take as Albert Bell.

Her father was ringing up the customer with the screws, so Frances walked over to the counter and waited impatiently until he carefully counted out the change and told the man to come back again.

"Dad," Frances burst out as soon as they were alone. "Did you know a dancing school is opening up right across the street?"

Mr. McAllister ran a hand through his thinning hair. "I do think I heard something about that."

"The sign is up already," Frances informed him.

Her father began writing down some figures. "Well, that's good," he said absently. "Might mean some more business for the town." Mr. McAllister was always worried about how few people shopped on Main Street.

"Dad," Frances said insistently, "Miss Leticia is going to give ballet lessons."

"I gather that means you'd like to take some then," her father said, looking up with a small smile.

"Well, yes. Can I?"

"Ask your mom, but I can't imagine she'd have any objections. Maybe Elizabeth would like to take lessons too."

Frances frowned. Elizabeth was eleven, two years older than Frances, and pretty good at just about everything she tried. Frances had the sinking feeling that if Elizabeth took ballet lessons, she'd be the one whirling across the stage. Frances would be where she always was—in the background, looking on enviously.

"Maybe she won't," Frances muttered, though she didn't see how anyone could resist ballet lessons.

"Are you going to hang around here for a while, honey?" her father asked.

Frances shook her head. "I'm going to meet Polly at Sadler's." Sadler's was Frances's favorite diner. "Mom told me to check in with you." Mrs. McAllister worked part time in the real-estate office across the street, but this afternoon she was off visiting her mother, Grammy Whitwell, who lived about an hour away.

"All right, consider yourself checked," Mr. McAllister said with a grin.

"Tell Mom I'll be home around three," Frances called on her way out the door.

Her father nodded, but his attention was back on his figures. From the frown on his face, Frances knew that he was adding up the week's business. It hadn't been very good lately.

Polly was already sitting in a booth by the time Frances walked into Sadler's. Polly Brock had moved to Lake Lister at the end of the summer and at first Frances hadn't liked her very much. She was bold and brassy, not at all like Frances's former best friend, Bonnie, who had moved away. But Polly was the kind of person who grew on you. She could be a tease, just like Albert Bell, but inside she was really very nice.

"Have you been here long?" Frances asked as she slid into the booth.

"Nope. I just got here."

The waitress, a woman of about fifty with bright blond hair that didn't look real, came over with menus.

"I don't need one," Frances said. "I'll have a grilled cheese sandwich and a glass of milk, please." She loved grilled cheese sandwiches, but her mother didn't make them right. She always burned one side.

"I guess I'll have grilled cheese," Polly said, "but with fries and a Coke. Some apple pie for dessert, too."

Frances was always amazed at how much Polly could eat. She wasn't fat, exactly, but she was broad. Frances thought if Polly lost a couple of pounds, she might be really pretty, with her dark curly hair and her bright brown eyes. Frances's eyes were brown, too, but they were kind of a muddy color. Her hair was a pretty shade of brown, but it was short, thanks to an unfortunate haircut. At least it was beginning to grow back now.

"Guess what, Polly," Frances said when the waitress left.

"What?"

"A ballet school is opening on Main Street."

Polly didn't seem very interested. "Yeah?"

"Don't you think that's wonderful?"

"What's so wonderful about it?"

"We can take ballet lessons."

"Ballet?" Polly hooted.

"Don't you think that would be fun?" Frances asked, disappointed.

"Can you see me galoomping around the dance floor?"

"You'd be learning, just like the rest of us beginners."

Polly shook her head. "Count me out."

Frances could feel all her old shyness returning. She wanted to take ballet, but she certainly didn't want to do it by herself. She had just assumed that Polly would be dancing right alongside her to give her confidence. Frances and Bonnie had always done things together. She wasn't ready to give up on the idea quite yet. "It would be fun," Frances argued. "Have you ever seen a ballet?"

"Of course. My father used to take me to *The Nutcracker* every Christmas when we lived in Milwaukee." As soon as Polly mentioned her father, she got a tight, hard look on her face. Her parents had gotten divorced last year, which was one of the reasons Mrs. Brock came to Lake Lister. She had taken a job as head of the local library.

Frances didn't know how to make Polly feel better about her father, whom she didn't see much, so instead she said, "Then you know how gorgeous a ballet can be. Can't you imagine being up there on stage?"

"No, I can't," Polly said bluntly.

Frances played with her fork. "Well, maybe Lena will take lessons with me." Lena Kroll had come to Lake Lister last year from an Eastern European country with a name that was hard to pronounce. Frances and Polly liked her a lot, but Lena's parents were strict, and the girls couldn't see her as much as they would have liked. She had to spend most of her time studying.

"Don't count on it. Mr. and Mrs. Kroll probably won't let her."

"I guess not," Frances said with a sigh. "Maybe I won't take lessons then either."

"Why not?" Polly demanded. "You should if you want to."

Frances could feel her stomach churning a little. "That snotty Tammi will probably be in the class . . . and some of the other girls . . . her friends . . ." Frances's voice trailed off.

Polly's voice softened. "Come on, Frances, you don't have to be scared around them. You've known them all your life."

"I know, but what if I don't do the steps right? Or I might fall down or something." Suddenly taking ballet lessons seemed rife with possibilities for looking stupid.

The waitress brought them their grilled cheese sandwiches. As Frances gloomily bit into hers, she said, "I think I'll wait until next year to take lessons."

"You mean you'd really let those girls keep you away?"

"They're not doing that. Exactly."

Polly gave her a shrewd look. "No?"

"It's dumb, I know," Frances said with embarrassment, "but I don't think I'd like it if I went alone."

Polly studied Frances's sad face. "Oh, what the

heck," she finally said. "I'll take ballet too, if it means that much to you."

"You will?" Frances replied in such a hopeful tone that Polly burst out laughing.

"Yes. But you have to do something for me."

"Anything," Frances said eagerly.

"You have to join the girls' basketball team with me. It's going to start practicing next week."

Frances looked at Polly in disbelief. "Basketball! You have to be tall for basketball."

"Not for grade-school basketball," Polly said, taking a sip of Coke. "They said anybody could join."

"I'm sure they didn't mean the smallest girl in the fourth grade," Frances muttered.

Polly shrugged. "That's the deal. You want me to keep you company, and I want the same thing."

Frances was about to say no. Basketball was gross; she didn't want any part of it. But to be fair, it was obvious Polly felt the same way about ballet. She thought longingly once more about the pretty pink satin slippers ballerinas got to wear. Weren't they worth an afternoon in the gym trying to throw a ball into a basket?

"All right," she said, her mind made up. "I'll do it."

"Shake," Polly said, sticking out a greasy hand.

Frances shook. But she wondered who was going to have a worse time, Polly huffing and puffing through ballet lessons, or her, the world's shortest basketball player.

2

frances came home that afternoon eager to share the news about Miss Leticia's School of the Dance with her mother. But Elizabeth had beat her to it. When Frances arrived, Elizabeth was already in the kitchen chattering to Mrs. McAllister about dancing.

"It's going to be great," she was saying enthusiastically. "I can start lessons, can't I?"

Mrs. McAllister laughed. "I suppose so." She turned to greet Frances. "Have you heard about the new dancing school?"

"Yes." But the wind had been taken out of her sails. Frances wanted to be the one to tell. Besides, she didn't want Elizabeth in ballet class with her.

Her mother looked at her curiously. "I thought you'd be more excited. You've been talking about ballet ever since we saw *Swan Lake*."

"I am excited," Frances said slowly.

Elizabeth poured herself a glass of milk. "Well, I don't want to take ballet lessons."

"You don't?" Frances and her mother asked practically in unison.

"No. I want to learn how to tap-dance." Elizabeth put her milk down on the table and did an impromptu shuffle. She wasn't very good, Frances was secretly pleased to see. Elizabeth definitely needed tap lessons.

"Well, I guess there's no reason you can't take tap if that's what you want," Mrs. McAllister said.

"Good," Elizabeth said. "I like it better than ballet. It's faster and more exciting."

Now that it seemed safe to assume that Elizabeth wouldn't be joining her at the ballet barre, Frances allowed herself to get more enthusiastic. "When do you think the school is going to open?" she asked.

"I'd say a few more weeks," Mrs. McAllister informed her.

"That long?" Frances responded, disappointed. "I saw the men working. The sign's already up."

"Miss Leticia is probably having a grand opening, and I haven't seen that advertised anywhere."

"Well, it can't be soon enough for me," Frances said fervently.

Almost every day after that Frances went down to Main Street and peered in the window. Sometimes she dragged Polly with her. Polly didn't like the idea of classes being held right in front of the big window where anyone could see them.

"It's . . . it's indecent," Polly sputtered. "We ought to have a little privacy, after all."

Despite her shyness, Frances didn't really mind the

idea of dancing in front of Main Street. Perhaps it would be embarrassing at first, but soon she'd be so good she'd barely notice her audience. Why, people would probably come from all around just to stand outside Miss Leticia's and watch her dance.

Frances wasn't the only one waiting for the dancing school to open. Many of the girls from Lake Lister Elementary were planning on taking ballet or tap. A few of the more adventurous said they were going to sign up for modern dance, even though they couldn't exactly say what that was.

One day Mr. McAllister came home with the local newspaper tucked under his arm. Frances and Elizabeth were up in their room finishing their homework. "I think there's something in *The Lake Lister Voice* that's going to interest you two," he told them.

Frances couldn't imagine what that might be. The newspaper was mostly ads. But an ad was just what her father wanted to show them. Paging through the paper, he finally stopped at a large advertisement for Miss Leticia's School of the Dance. Both girls grabbed for it.

"Hey, hey," Mr. McAllister said, holding the newspaper over his head. "Let's calm down here. We'll read it together."

He sat down on Frances's bed—the neatly made-up bed, unlike Elizabeth's messy pile of blanket, spread, and pillows on the other side of the room. Frances and Elizabeth curled up on either side of him.

To Frances's delight there was a drawing of a ballerina prominently displayed in the corner. Frances checked her out—tutu, toe shoes with ribbons that wrapped around the dancer's slender ankles, and hair that was piled on her head in a neat bun.

"Another reason I shouldn't have gotten my hair cut," Frances muttered. But she quickly moved over to the copy, which proclaimed OPEN HOUSE in bold letters. It went on to invite the residents of Lake Lister and surrounding communities to visit the "outstanding facilities" at Miss Leticia's School of the Dance on Saturday.

"There's going to be punch and cookies," Elizabeth read.

"And a ten percent discount for anyone who signs up on the day of the open house," Frances added.

"Pretty clever marketing idea," Mr. McAllister commented.

"Can we sign up on Saturday?" Frances asked, her eyes shining.

"I don't think we could make you wait any longer if we wanted to," her father said, laughing.

At dinner Mrs. McAllister agreed that the girls should sign up on Saturday. "I'll come with you. And I'll bring my checkbook," she added with a sigh. "You know, girls, these lessons might have to be part of your Christmas gifts."

Elizabeth and Frances exchanged looks. They knew that business at the hardware store wasn't very good. Money was getting tight.

"That's all right, Mom," Elizabeth said, using her mature voice as she helped herself to some fried chicken. "We understand."

"I think you're wasting your money, Mom," Mike

said, grabbing a couple of drumsticks. "These two can't dance."

"Mike," Mr. McAllister said over his daughters' howls of protest, "that's not very nice."

Mike shrugged. "I can't help it if I'm the only one who can see things clearly around here. These two are the klutz sisters."

"All right, all right. That's enough," Mrs. McAllister intervened. "I have some news too."

Everyone looked at her expectantly. "Not only will Grammy be joining us for Thanksgiving, but Aunt Nan and Uncle Otto and Sissy and Roy are coming too."

This announcement was met with silence. Aunt Nan and Uncle Otto were fine, but their children, Sissy and Roy, were spoiled brats in the McAllister kids' opinion. Sissy was a year older than Elizabeth, and all she talked about was boys, boys, boys. Roy was just eight. Chubby, with glasses, Roy thought he was the smartest eight-year-old in the history of the world. Maybe he was; he certainly knew all about current events and read lots of books. That would be all right if he wasn't always so eager to show off his smarts and make everyone else feel stupid in comparison.

Both Sissy and Roy were whiners of the first order as well. Even though Aunt Nan and her family lived in Milwaukee, about an hour's drive, the McAllisters only saw them a couple times a year. Even that seemed like a lot.

"Well, can't you say something?" Mrs. McAllister seemed hurt.

"Can you pass the mashed potatoes?" Mike inquired.

Mrs. McAllister shoved the bowl in his direction. "I think it would be nice if you were a little friendlier to Sissy and Roy this year. They are the only cousins you have, after all."

Thank goodness, Frances thought. She didn't think she could handle any more like Sissy and Roy. Then Frances had an idea—something that might make Thanksgiving a little more fun.

"I was talking to Polly the other day. She was supposed to go to visit her father for Thanksgiving, but he said he was going out of town. Could we invite her and her mother?"

"I don't see why not," Mrs. McAllister replied. "If they don't have other plans."

"They don't. Polly said they'd probably wind up eating out."

"Well, then, let's have them over for sure. I'll call Mrs. Brock later."

"Thanks, Mom." Frances beamed at her. With Polly around, Sissy and Roy wouldn't dare start up.

Frances always saved a place for Polly on the bus. As soon as Polly climbed aboard the next day, Frances waved her over. "My mom told me this morning you're definitely coming for Thanksgiving."

"Yeah," Polly said glumly. "We'll be there."

"Well, don't sound so happy about it," Frances said, offended.

"Oh, I'm glad." Polly was immediately contrite. "It's just that I really counted on seeing my dad."

Frances traced a pattern on the leg of her jeans. Polly didn't like to talk about her dad, but Frances could tell how much her friend missed him.

"How come he had to cancel?" Frances finally asked.

"He's got some business in Atlanta on Friday morning, so he said it would just be easier to postpone our visit until Christmas. He's very busy right now," Polly said defensively.

Even though Polly had explained it to her, Frances was never quite sure what Mr. Brock did for a living. He owned several companies, Frances knew, and he always seemed to be traveling around doing business in some part of the country.

"Say, did you see the ad in the paper for Miss Leticia's grand opening?" Frances asked, eager to change the subject.

Polly made a face. "No."

"Well, it's going to be Saturday," Frances said, ignoring Polly's pained expression.

"You know, I've been thinking, Frances . . ."

"You promised!" Frances said accusingly.

"I didn't exactly promise."

Frances gave Polly a baleful look. "You shook on it."

"All right. I guess it would be kind of creepy of me to back out now."

"It sure would."

"Okay, okay, I'll go through with it. You're just lucky Mr. Robinson's been out of commission."

Mr. Robinson was the gym teacher who was going to coach the girls' basketball team. He had been out of school for a week with the flu, so sign-up for the basketball team had been postponed.

"Ballet for you, basketball for me." Frances stuck

out her hand and the girls shook on it. "We've shaken on it twice now. You can't back out."

"I won't," Polly said with a sigh.

"Good." A small smile lit up Frances's face. "We'll sign up on Saturday."

By the time Saturday arrived, Frances was in agony trying to figure out the right thing to wear to the open house. Though she was normally neat, Frances had pulled everything out of her closet and strewn it across her bed. Now she wrinkled her nose at the jeans, sweaters, and blouses. Nothing seemed good enough to wear on such a momentous day.

"What's this?" Elizabeth said, coming into the room, her eyes wide. Frances was usually yelling at *her* for making a mess.

"My entire wardrobe."

Elizabeth sat down on her bed, which, while unmade, looked positively neat compared with Frances's. "I figured that. Why isn't it in your closet?"

"I'm trying to find something to wear to the open house." Frances looked her sister over. "You're not planning on going in that, are you?"

Elizabeth looked down at herself. She was wearing corduroy pants and a University of Wisconsin sweatshirt with a big badger on it. "Why not?"

"Don't you think you should wear something a little more . . . more . . ." Frances searched for a word. "Dancerish?"

"Gee, my lace ball gown is at the cleaners," Elizabeth replied sarcastically.

"Well, I'm not going to Miss Leticia's dressed in

regular clothes," Frances said stoutly. She wanted to make a good impression, to have Miss Leticia see that she was serious about dancing. "Don't you have anything I could borrow?"

"Frances, you know all my clothes are too big on you."

That was one of the problems with being so short. She and Elizabeth couldn't even borrow each other's clothes.

"Wait, I have an idea," Elizabeth said, snapping her fingers. She went to the back of her closet and pulled out a skirt. "Remember when I bought this miniskirt and Mom told me it was indecent? It should be just the right length for you."

It was a pretty turquoise color, and Frances tried it on with a lace-collared blouse. Looking at herself from different angles in the closet mirror, she liked what she saw. With her patent-leather shoes she'd be ready to twirl off. "Perfect," she said. "Thanks, Elizabeth."

Elizabeth waved her hand. "No problem. But I'm still wearing this."

Another person who chose not to dress up was Polly. She came to the door wearing her oldest jeans and a sweater so stretched out it looked like it might almost fit one of the Green Bay Packers. Frances didn't say anything to Polly about her outfit. Despite their handshake, Frances knew she was lucky that Polly was coming at all.

Elizabeth had already left to meet her friend Ellen, but Frances and Polly were going to swing by Lena's house, so she could join them at the open house too.

"I don't know why Lena wants to come along if she can't take lessons," Polly said, her voice fading into the blustery wind.

"She just wants to see what the school is like."

Certainly after getting Lena, it was clear that she was a lot more excited than Polly about going to the open house.

"Let's hurry," she said in her slightly accented voice.

Polly wanted to hurry, too, but just because she was cold.

When they arrived at Miss Leticia's School of the Dance, the open house was in full swing. The big practice room was filled with girls of all ages and their mothers. There wasn't a boy or father in sight. Frances looked around warily to see if Albert Bell was anywhere on the premises. He didn't seem to be, so Frances breathed a sigh of relief and set out to enjoy herself.

"What do we do?" Lena asked in a nervous whisper.

"Have some food," Polly said decisively, and headed for the punch and cookies.

Frances, however, stood in the middle of the room and looked around. It was just a room, empty except for an upright piano in the corner, but the wooden floor had a polished, shiny look that said "Dance on me." Behind the bars lining the room were mirrors that reflected the crowd talking and enjoying their refreshments.

"Should we introduce ourselves to Miss Leticia?" Lena asked.

"Which one is she?"

"Over there."

"Oh." She was hidden behind a group of mothers, but there was only one woman in the room who could be Miss Leticia. For one thing, she was wearing a pink leotard and a skirt made of filmy material in the same rosy color. Her dark, glossy hair was swept into a knot on top of her head. If her outfit hadn't given her away, her manner would have. She seemed perfectly in control of the room as she talked brightly, her delicate hands gesturing here and there.

Frances looked at Miss Leticia and felt her shyness dripping down to her toes. "I don't think so, Lena."

Polly sauntered up to them, a paper cup of punch in one hand, a plate of cookies in the other. "Good eats," she said, so Frances and Lena went off to get some food too. Frances almost bumped into her sister at the refreshment table.

"Mom should be here any time to sign us up," Elizabeth said, grabbing a napkin.

"You don't think we'll have to meet Miss Leticia, do you?" Frances asked.

Elizabeth eyed her sister curiously. "Not if you don't want to. You're going to have to talk to her eventually, though."

"Oh, I know." But she didn't want to meet this glamorous woman right now. Not with all these people around.

As it turned out, she needn't have worried. Mrs. McAllister arrived a few moments later and was in a hurry. She signed up both girls at a desk where a woman was taking money, had a quick glass of punch and a look around, then said to Frances and Elizabeth, "Get your friends so I can drive them home. It's going to snow."

Frances didn't want to leave, but she dutifully went to get Lena and Polly. Once she was in the car she asked her mother, "When do the lessons start?"

"Ballet on the Tuesday after Thanksgiving, tap on Thursday."

Just a little more than a week! Frances thought.

That night as she lay in bed trying to sleep, Frances thought about the Sugar Plum Fairy from *The Nutcracker*. Frances had never seen that ballet, but she loved the sound of the words "Sugar Plum Fairy." She could imagine what the dancer must look like, wearing a dress like cotton candy and shiny sprinkles in her hair. Drifting off to sleep, Frances could see herself as the Sugar Plum Fairy, twirling around the dance floor. It wouldn't be long now.

3

frances could smell Thanksgiving before she even opened her eyes. Wafting through the heating vent came the delicious aroma of pumpkin pies baking in the oven.

She rolled over in her bed, hoping that she would fall back to sleep and dream she was having a big slice of pie with whipped cream on top. Instead she felt a big arm giving her a shake.

"What . . . Oh, Mike, what do you want?" she groaned.

"Mom wants you up," her brother said authoritatively. "Uncle Otto and Aunt Nan and the little Zits should be here soon." Their relatives' last name was actually Ritz, but Mike had nicknamed them the Zits—out of Mr. and Mrs. McAllister's hearing range, of course. He said Sissy and Roy were like pimples, always turning up when you didn't want them.

Without waiting for Frances to get out of bed, Mike went over to give Elizabeth a nudge. She had already heard the commotion, however, and was sitting up.

"It's only eight thirty," Elizabeth said, glancing at the clock. "It's a holiday, for heaven's sake."

"Tell it to Mom. I think she wants you to peel potatoes." He laughed as he left the room. Mike knew that it was Elizabeth's least favorite job.

The girls straggled out of bed and got dressed. Once Frances had washed her face and brushed her hair, she was eager to get downstairs. Even with the Zits coming, Thanksgiving was still Frances's favorite holiday. Christmas had presents, but Thanksgiving had a cozy family feeling that Frances loved.

"Good morning, honey," her mother greeted her.

Mrs. McAllister looked as if she had been cooking for a week and not just a morning. Her hair had bits of flour sticking to it, and the apron that covered her blouse and slacks already showed a few spots.

"Did you put the turkey in yet?" Frances asked.

"Oh, no. It would get done too soon. All I've really finished are the pies. I wanted to get those out of the way before the company arrives so we can have a little time to visit." She glanced at her watch. "They should be here by noon at the latest. The next thing I'd like to get out of the way is the potatoes. You can help me peel them."

Frances made a face. She didn't like peeling any more than Elizabeth did, though she certainly enjoyed the fluffy mounds of mashed potatoes when her mother served them at dinner. "Why don't I feed Snowflake first?" she suggested. Snowflake was Frances's kitten, and Frances took very good care of her.

"Fine," Mrs. McAllister said, "but that doesn't mean you won't have to peel potatoes, too."

Frances sighed. It was hard to put anything past her mother. As she put fresh water into Snowflake's bowl, Frances asked, "What time is dinner?"

"Oh, probably around four."

"Four! What time is Polly coming?"

"I told her mother about three."

That was bad news. It meant Sissy and Roy might be around at least three hours before Polly showed up. "Can I ask Polly to come over earlier?"

Mrs. McAllister shrugged. "If it's all right with her mother. Before you do the potatoes, why don't you start setting the table?"

"What about Elizabeth?"

"She'll help."

"If she ever gets down here," Frances muttered. She knew all of her sister's tricks. Right now Elizabeth was taking the world's longest shower, and by the time she walked into the dining room the job would be done, and she'd be full of excuses. Sure enough, ten minutes later, just as Frances was laying out the napkins, Elizabeth sauntered in.

"Where have you been?" Frances asked.

Mike, who was passing through the dining room with a stack of old magazines his mother had asked him to get rid of, answered for Elizabeth. "Turkey. Get it? A Thanksgiving pun."

"Oh, Mike, grow up," Elizabeth said disdainfully. She held up her finger. It had a pretty pink bandage around it, the only kind Elizabeth would wear. "I got a paper cut."

"Gee, I hope you'll live," Mike said sarcastically as he headed into the kitchen.

"I hope you'll be well enough to help with all the work we've got to do around here," Frances added.

Elizabeth beamed at her sister. "Well, it looks like setting the table is all done."

"But I still haven't peeled the potatoes," Frances said brightly.

A few moments later they both had peelers in hand and were attacking a stack of potatoes that seemed as high as a skyscraper.

"It's so nice that you girls are old enough to help now," Mrs. McAllister said as she sipped a cup of coffee. She told the girls she was having "a well-deserved break."

"We've always helped, haven't we?" Elizabeth asked. "It sure seems like it."

Mrs. McAllister laughed. "I remember when you were four and Frances was two. The stuffing was made, ready to be put into the turkey, and I left the kitchen for a few minutes. By the time I got back, you both were covered with stuffing. Elizabeth, you informed me that since there wasn't enough snow for a good snowball fight, you decided to throw the stuffing at each other."

"I think I remember that," Elizabeth murmured.

"You should. It was the last time I spanked you." Mrs. McAllister shook her head. "That was some holiday. The company was expected in an hour, and I spent most of that time bathing you two."

"Well, I promise no snowball fights with the stuffing this year," Elizabeth said.

Mrs. McAllister smiled. "No, this will be a nice quiet holiday with friends and family." She looked at her watch. "In fact, your father should be back with Grammy any time now."

As if on cue, Mr. McAllister and Grammy Whitwell, carrying several shopping bags, walked in the front door. Everyone went to greet them, and there were hugs all around.

"Let me take your coat, Mom," Mrs. McAllister said.

"All right. Jeannie, I made cookies and a vegetable casserole and, oh, yes, soup . . ."

"Mom, I told you you didn't have to make anything."

Grammy's blue eyes sparkled. "I know, I know, but I have to have a little fun too."

Frances thought Grammy was the perfect kind of grandmother. For one thing she wasn't too young. Frances thought grandmothers should have white hair and be round and cozy, which described Grammy perfectly. She was also the sort of grandmother who baked and worked in the garden and liked to buy her grandchildren presents, all of which Frances found very satisfactory.

After Grammy had kissed all of them several times (even Mike submitted to this) and put her things away in the basement guest room, she came into the kitchen and put on an apron. "What's next?" she asked.

"Oh, Mom, the girls and I have it under control," Mrs. McAllister said.

Grammy ignored her daughter. "What about the turkey? Don't you want to get it in?"

Mrs. McAllister glanced at her watch. "In about

fifteen minutes. We could do the biscuit dough, I guess."

But before they could get started, the doorbell rang. It was the Ritz family, and to the McAllisters' surprise, they had a dog with them. And not just any dog, either—this was a big white furry Samoyed, whose name, predictably, was Sammy.

"Isn't he adorable?" Aunt Nan said as she went around her circle of relatives, hugging each one. "We just got him last week."

"He belonged to one of my employees at the factory," Uncle Otto informed them. "They couldn't keep him anymore, so we decided to take him."

Sissy had given Grammy a chaste kiss, but now she stood in the doorway, looking around the living room with distaste. The Ritzes had recently moved into a larger house in a suburb outside of Milwaukee. Frances hadn't seen it yet, but from the expression on Sissy's face, she obviously thought it much nicer than this one. Roy, on the other hand, was busy trying to control Sammy, who was almost as big as he was.

Mr. and Mrs. McAllister looked at each other. Then Mr. McAllister started rubbing his eyes. He was allergic to most dogs and cats, and Frances was lucky her dad liked Snowflake so much, or she never would have been allowed to keep her. He tolerated some sneezing around Snowflake. However, Mr. McAllister didn't look as though he cared much for Sammy.

Clearing her throat, Mrs. McAllister said, "You know, Nan, Jim is allergic to dogs."

"Is he? Well, I guess we could keep him in the car," she said doubtfully.

"We could tie him up outside," Uncle Otto said, "but he barks plenty."

"Oh, that's all right." Mr. McAllister tried to sound hearty. "I'll just stay away from him." Then he sneezed.

The grownups sat down to talk for a while, and Mike loped off to watch a football game on television. That left Elizabeth and Frances to entertain Sissy and Roy.

"Would you like to play Monopoly?" Elizabeth asked politely.

Sissy very slightly shook her head, as if to say, What a silly idea. "Don't you have Trivial Pursuit?" Roy piped up. "I'm excellent at that."

Before Frances could answer, the doorbell rang again. Polly opened the door and came inside before anyone could answer it. "Hi," she greeted everyone.

"I'm really glad you're here," Frances said fervently.

Polly's eyes widened. "What's that?" she asked, pointing at Sammy.

"A dog," Roy replied seriously. "A Samoyed. Originally they're from Siberia. They're related to chows and spitzes."

Polly warily patted Sammy on the head. When he made a small lunge in her direction, she took a few steps backward.

"We were all about to—" Frances stopped. What were they about to do?

"I guess we could all go up to our room," Elizabeth suggested unhappily.

"What will we do there?" Sissy asked in her superior voice.

Frances shrugged. "Talk, I guess."

"Or we could play Trivial Pursuit," Roy chattered away as they climbed the stairs. "If you have it. You never said."

"We don't," Elizabeth said bluntly.

It was a little difficult for all of them to fit into Frances and Elizabeth's room. Even though the girls had cleaned up for the company, and Elizabeth's bed was made (for once), there wasn't much room for them to sit down. Polly and Frances squashed in on Frances's bed, Elizabeth sat on hers, Sissy took the rocker, and Roy dropped down on the floor. Sammy almost sat on top of him.

"So is Lake Lister as exciting as ever?" Sissy asked, smoothing down her suede skirt, which barely came to her knees.

"A dancing school is opening," Frances said.

Sissy raised one eyebrow. "Really? Here?"

"Yes, here," Elizabeth replied, irritated.

"Sounds like fun," Sissy replied, making it sound anything but.

Roy got up and began pawing through the books on the girls' shelves. "Don't you have an encyclopedia? We do. I'm reading it all the way through. I'm already on N."

The whole time Roy was talking, Sammy was circling the small room, his tail swishing around.

"Can't you make him sit down?" Polly asked irritably.

Roy made an attempt to grab Sammy. "Don't you like dogs?"

"I like dogs. This looks more like a wolf."

"So," Sissy said, turning to Elizabeth, "are you dating anyone yet?"

"I'm not allowed to date," Elizabeth replied primly.

"Really?" There was an amused note in Sissy's voice. "My boyfriend and I go to the movies all the time."

"You mean you go with your girlfriends," Roy corrected. "And the boys sit behind you."

Frances and Polly looked at each other and rolled their eyes. Now it was Elizabeth's turn to sound amused. "Oh, *that* kind of dating. Sure, we do that."

Sammy jumped up and started licking Sissy's face. "Get out of here," she said angrily as she pushed him away.

Maybe it was the tone of Sissy's voice, but Sammy did take off. In fact, he galloped out of the bedroom, knocking over a wastepaper basket as he went.

"You'd better get him," Elizabeth warned. "He could do a lot of damage."

Roy jumped up, and the others followed. They rushed downstairs just as Snowflake was darting across Sammy's path. The sight of that white ball of fur made Sammy even wilder. Suddenly he was chasing after the cat, and they were both headed for the kitchen.

Frances arrived at the kitchen door in time to see it all. A terrified Snowflake streaked past Grammy, who was carrying the turkey to the oven. Sammy was hot on her tail, and Grammy stumbled over him,

dropping the turkey and its pan, which clattered to the floor. Grammy pitched forward, knocking over the garbage can and falling to the floor herself.

"Oww!" Grammy cried, grabbing her ankle. Frances ran over to her and helped her up. Wincing in pain, she hobbled over to a chair.

Mrs. McAllister and the rest of the adults ran in from the living room where they had been talking. "What happened?"

"My ankle," Grammy moaned. "I've done something to it."

"It was Sammy," Frances burst out. "He knocked her over."

"No, it wasn't," Roy said, pushing his way over to his grandmother, whose face was twisted with pain. "It was that cat of yours. She started it."

"Enough!" bellowed Mr. McAllister.

Frances's mother, who was examining the ankle, said grimly, "We've got to take you to the hospital, Mom. It might be broken."

"No, no," Grammy protested. "It's probably just a sprain."

"We can't take that chance," Aunt Nan said, putting her hand on her mother's shoulder.

"All right, if we must."

Mr. McAllister and Uncle Otto rushed over to help Grammy get up. "Someone clean up that turkey," Mr. McAllister said. "We don't want anyone else to trip."

"I want to go the hospital too," Roy said, his eyes filling with tears. He didn't look like a boy genius now, Frances thought, just a kid who was feeling bad about his grandmother.

"No, you stay here," Aunt Nan told him.

"All of you kids stay here," Mrs. McAllister said.

"I'll watch them," Mike said quietly.

In a few minutes the adults were ready to leave. Mr. McAllister and Uncle Otto made a seat with their hands to carry Grammy out to the car. She tried to smile reassuringly at the children, but there were tears in her eyes.

As soon as the door slammed shut, Elizabeth turned angrily to Sissy and Roy. "Now see what you did with that dumb dog of yours? Where is he, anyway?"

"He's not dumb," Roy insisted.

"If your cat hadn't frightened him . . ." Sissy began, sticking up for her brother for once.

"That cat belongs here," Frances cut in.

Mike put his fingers in his mouth and gave a sharp whistle. Everyone turned to look at him. "Cut it out."

"But—" Roy objected.

"Enough," Mike said, looking as though he meant it. "Snowflake is hiding somewhere, and Sammy is curled up in front of the fireplace. Let's leave well enough alone." He glanced around the kitchen. "Dad was right, though. We'd better do something about this."

Frances looked at the turkey in the middle of the kitchen floor. Lying on its back, its wings and legs spread out, it looked like an undressed doll with its head cut off. Even worse, it was covered with potato peelings and other garbage. The stuffing had spilled out of it, too, and was all over the floor. "The turkey is ruined!" she cried.

Just then Sammy raced back into the kitchen and started licking the stuffing up with his big tongue. Then before anyone could stop him, he dragged the bird off into the corner and started tearing off bits of it with his teeth.

"Hey," Mike said in a loud voice, running over to the dog. "Get out of there."

Sammy struggled, but Mike finally pulled him away and got him out of the kitchen. The kids ran over to look at the naked, demolished bird.

"Ugh!" Elizabeth made a gagging noise.

Mike came over. "It's certainly ruined now."

"Don't you think we'd better clean this mess up?" Polly asked practically.

"Yeah, I do." Frances looked at Elizabeth, who looked at Sissy.

"All right, I'll do it," Sissy said defiantly. "Get me a garbage bag."

Mike held open the bag while Roy helped Sissy, who was making a face, pick up the turkey and shove it into the bag. "There goes dinner," Mike said.

Elizabeth nodded. "You're right. What are we going to do now?"

"Well, the first thing we should do is wash the floor." Mike grabbed some paper towels, dampened them in the sink, and tossed them around. Quietly everyone began cleaning up the stuffing, the garbage, and in general straightening up.

As Frances finished wiping down the counters, she said, "What do we want to do about dinner?"

"Maybe we could go out to a restaurant," Elizabeth suggested.

"Are any open around here?" Sissy asked skeptically.

There were several nice restaurants that were serving Thanksgiving dinner, but when Mike called for reservations they were too full to take such a big party. "We'll just have to pull something together here," Mike said.

"But what?" Elizabeth asked.

Mike began rummaging through the freezer. "We have lots of hamburger, and there's hot dogs in the fridge."

"Hamburgers and hot dogs?" Sissy made a face.

"I love hamburgers," Roy said happily. "I hate turkey."

"We have the pies." Elizabeth began ticking off items. "And the potatoes are already boiled. We can stick them in the fridge until they're ready to be microwaved and mashed. There's also the soup and the vegetable casserole that Grammy brought."

"How *is* Grammy? Why haven't we heard anything?" Frances felt her lips start to tremble.

Polly went over and put her arm around Frances. "Let's call my mom. Maybe she can find out about your grandmother."

When Mrs. Brock heard what was happening at the McAllisters', she hurried over. By then the kids were all working together fixing a dinner, with only the occasional protest from Sissy. She hated mashing the potatoes as much as Elizabeth and Frances hated peeling them.

"You kids have done a great job," Mrs. Brock marveled. "And I think we should eat. I'm sure you're all famished."

"What about my grandmother?" Frances asked. "Can we call the hospital?"

"I'll do it now," Mrs. Brock promptly said.

But before she could even pick up the phone, Mr. and Mrs. McAllister, Aunt Nan, and Uncle Otto came in, pushing Grammy in a wheelchair.

There was a flurry as everyone rushed to the door. "What happened?" Frances asked.

"I did break my ankle," Grammy said, accepting a kiss from Elizabeth. "So stupid of me."

"So stupid of that dog," Frances muttered.

"Come on, let's go into the living room and sit down," Mrs. McAllister said, shepherding them out of the hallway.

"Luckily it wasn't very busy at the hospital," Aunt Nan said. "They said Grammy will be fine."

Sammy slunk over to Grammy and put his head in her lap. When he looked up at her with his big brown eyes as if to say "Sorry," everyone laughed.

"Well, this has turned out to be quite a Thanksgiving," Mrs. McAllister said, rubbing her forehead. "And just this morning I was complaining about a food fight that Elizabeth and Frances had years ago."

"Speaking of food, I'm starving," Mr. McAllister said. "What are we going to eat?"

"The kids have taken care of all that," Mrs. Brock said. "We were just about to throw some hamburgers and hot dogs on the gas grill. We may not have turkey, but we have all the trimmings."

"Sounds great!" Mr. McAllister said fervently.

When everyone finally sat down around the table with its wide variety of food, Mr. McAllister said, "We have a lot to be thankful for. Grammy's going to be all right, we're all together, and we've got plenty to eat—even if this does look a little more like the Fourth of July than Thanksgiving!"

4

"What an interesting holiday you had," Lena said, taking a bite of her sandwich. It was the first day back at school after vacation.

"That's one word for it." Frances unwrapped her own sandwich. Bologna. At least it wasn't turkey leftovers like it usually was for a week after Thanksgiving. "I guess it was fun after the bad stuff was over. By the time my cousins went home with their dog, though, my dad was sneezing all over the place. My aunt and uncle were *really* sorry they brought him."

"Your cousin Roy isn't too bad, but Sissy . . ." Polly made a face.

"I heard her asking Mike if he had friends in Milwaukee. Boy friends, to fix her up with. He just laughed."

Stirring her straw around in her milk, Polly said, "Your grandma's awfully nice. It seemed like a real family with everyone sitting around the table and all."

"Well, of course it is," Frances said with surprise. Then she realized what Polly meant. She didn't have a real family anymore. "You're going to see your dad at Christmas, aren't you?"

Polly shrugged. "I don't know. I'm supposed to."

Frances and Lena exchanged glances. Polly was usually so cheerful. Now she suddenly looked as if she had a stomachache.

"So when do your dancing lessons begin?" Lena asked, changing the subject.

"Tomorrow," Frances and Polly said in unison, though one of them sounded elated and the other glum.

Lena sighed. "I wish I could go too."

"You asked your parents?"

"Many times. If I keep my grades high, they said maybe in the spring."

"I can sell you a leotard cheap," Polly murmured.

"Come on, Polly," Frances scolded. "You're going in with a bad attitude."

"Yep," Polly agreed. "But at least I'm going."

The next day Frances wondered if Polly was going after all. When the bell rang, Frances was almost the first one out the classroom door. She had to turn around several times to see if Polly was behind her. She wasn't. Finally Frances spotted her at her locker.

"We're going to be late," she said after bucking the exiting crowd and making her way back to Polly. "Hurry," Frances begged.

"It only takes ten minutes to walk downtown, and we've got a half hour," Polly said, pulling up the hood of her parka.

"But we want to have plenty of time to get into our leotards."

"That's going to take me every spare minute," Polly said bluntly. "Mine barely fits."

Everyone who had signed up with Miss Leticia had received a photocopied letter of welcome in the mail. The same drawing of the ballerina that appeared in the ad was on the letterhead. She was on Elizabeth's letter, too, even though Elizabeth was taking tap. Frances liked that. It must mean that Miss Leticia, like Frances, thought the only real kind of dancing was ballet.

In the letter Miss Leticia had instructed the new students what they should bring the first day. Beginning ballet needed one black leotard, one pair of black ballet slippers, one pair of black tights, and one towel.

Since the first two items were not the kind of thing you could find at Crawford's, Mrs. Brock had driven the girls out to the mall on Saturday to see what they could come up with. Frances wished fervently that she could substitute some other color for black, pink, maybe, but she didn't have the nerve to go against Miss Leticia's requests.

They tried the big department store without any luck, but one of the saleswomen directed them to a lingerie shop.

Both Frances and Polly started giggling when they walked through the door. Hanging from pink padded hangers in every color imaginable were bras, and lots of them. Some seemed very large.

"Girls," Mrs. Brock hissed. "Act your age. You've seen underwear before."

At the word "underwear," the girls started giggling again.

"I'll leave you here," Mrs. Brock warned.

That sobered up Frances, but Polly had to put her hand over her mouth as they walked by a display of girdles.

Mrs. Brock told the woman behind the counter what they were looking for, and in short order she produced two black leotards, one in the smallest size she had, the other in the largest.

"They're so plain," Frances murmured as the woman wrapped them.

Mrs. Brock laughed. "You don't start out in a tutu, you know."

Actually Frances didn't know. A tutu was exactly what she was hoping for.

Fortunately the shoe store carried the ballet slippers and tights Miss Leticia wanted, so except for her towel, Frances was ready. When she got home, she found the perfect towel, white with pink flowers, and packed it and the rest of her gear in a tote bag, ready to bring to school.

Now that the big moment had finally arrived, however, Frances could feel herself getting a little nervous. What if she wasn't any good at ballet?

"How come you're just standing there staring into space?" Polly demanded, slamming her locker door.

"I'm not." She didn't want to further discourage Polly, who, Frances knew, would happily cut the class at the slightest sign of weakness. "Let's go. We really are going to be late."

Frances had heard that a number of the girls at her school were taking beginning ballet, but she was surprised to see just how many there were. When she and Polly arrived at Miss Leticia's, the dressing room was spilling over with girls in various stages of undress.

Elizabeth had informed Frances that the older beginners' ballet had a class of their own—Elizabeth's friends were scheduled on Mondays. Frances had been afraid that there might be some little kids today, but she was pleased to see that almost everyone looked as if they were in the third, fourth, or fifth grade.

"There's Tammi," Polly said with a sniff.

Tammi thought she was the coolest kid in the fourth grade. Actually Frances thought that, too. Tammi was surrounded by a few of her friends, who were admiring her ballet slippers, which were pink.

"How come she gets to wear pink?" Frances demanded indignantly.

Polly shrugged as she hung up her coat on one of the wooden hooks that ran along the wall. "Maybe she got special permission."

"I don't see why," Frances mumbled. She pulled her black slippers out of her tote. Suddenly they didn't seem quite so special anymore.

Though there was lots of noise around them, Frances and Polly undressed quietly. The only furniture in the changing room was a bench that ran the length of it. Frances hung up her coat on one of the hooks above the bench, neatly folded her school clothes, and put them in her tote.

Polly, on the other hand, left her garments in a heap on the floor. She looked around to see if anyone was noticing her dressed only in underpants and undershirt. No one was, except Frances.

"Saturday," Frances said.

"Huh?"

"Your underpants have Saturday written on them."

Polly looked down at the blue script flowing across the leg of her white panties. "Yeah, I have a pair for every day of the week. That's the kind of present my grandmother gives me."

"Then why aren't you wearing Tuesday?" Frances asked.

"Frances," Polly said, exasperated, "I do my own laundry. It's hard enough making sure I have clean underwear in my drawer. I can't always count on wearing the right day."

That summed up the difference between them, Frances thought as she slipped into her leotard. She would never be caught with the wrong day on. It would make her feel uncomfortable all day knowing she was sporting a Friday when it was really Thursday.

Tammi walked over to them, followed by Sheila and Leslie, two girls from their class. Tammi's hair was pulled back into a bun like the ballet dancer on Miss Leticia's stationery. Earlier in the year, when Frances had cut her hair, it was because she'd heard that all the really cool girls were wearing it short. Apparently no one had told Tammi. She looked just the way Frances wanted to.

Tammi gave Frances and Polly the once-over.

"What are you looking at?" Polly said bluntly.

"Nothing. I'm just surprised you're taking ballet, Polly."

"Frankly, so am I."

"You don't seem like the type."

Sheila and Leslie giggled, as if on cue.

"Well, at least I'm wearing the regulation outfit." Polly gave a significant glance in the direction of Tammi's pink shoes.

"Miss Leticia won't mind once she sees me dance."

Before Polly could retort, one of the girls scurried in from the main room. "We're ready to start," she reported breathlessly.

In a few minutes the class had assembled in the classroom. They stood huddled together, but Miss Leticia was nowhere to be seen. The only other person in the room was a heavyset middle-aged woman at the piano, looking bored.

"Bonjour, girls." Miss Leticia fluttered in from her office. "That means 'Good day' in French. Can you repeat?"

The girls all said *bonjour,* though hardly in unison.

"Well, it is a good day. Our very first ballet class."

Frances looked at Miss Leticia with satisfaction. Anyone who saw her would know she was a ballet teacher. Like the girls, she wore a leotard, but it was bright blue. With it she wore blue tights and soft, pale blue ballet slippers. Her raven-colored hair was tied behind her with a white ribbon.

"I'd like to introduce you to Mrs. Morton." The lady at the piano nodded and ran one hand down the length of the keys. It made an impressive sound. "She will be our accompanist, and for right now, I'd like her to play a happy song while we get acquainted."

Mrs. Morton nodded and began playing "If You're

Happy and You Know It, Clap Your Hands." Frances had learned that song in preschool and thought it was highly inappropriate for a ballet class, but Miss Leticia, who was swaying in time to the music, didn't seem to notice.

"Now, the first thing I'm going to do is take attendance. It will be a while before I learn your names," she warned, "but soon I hope to know you all."

Miss Leticia went over to the piano, where her clipboard was lying. One by one she began checking off names, and as she did so, she directed each girl to a place at the barre. Frances soon figured out that Miss Leticia was arranging the girls by their height. Frances knew where that left her. Right at the front. It made her nervous to think everyone standing behind her could watch her dance.

Once attendance had been taken and the girls were all arranged, Miss Leticia clapped her hands together. "We begin ballet with the five positions. I will now demonstrate first position."

Miss Leticia put her feet together, then turned them out so the heels were touching. "First position. Now you try it."

It looked easy enough when Miss Leticia did it, but when Frances tried to turn her feet out, they felt as if they might be breaking a little at the ankles.

Miss Leticia started up the line. "Relax your feet, dear," she said, patting Frances on the shoulder.

Frances didn't understand how she could do that and first position, too. If she relaxed her feet, they would go right back to the way they always were, toes forward instead of sideways.

Once Miss Leticia passed her, Frances cautiously turned her head to see how the other students were doing. Polly was way back at the end of the line, so Frances couldn't catch a glimpse of her. But she did have a good view of Tammi, who was smiling widely. Obviously her toes didn't mind facing east and west. Frances was pleased, though, when she heard Miss Leticia pass Tammi and say quietly, "Oh, dear, I thought I made it clear. The slippers are supposed to be black."

The next positions weren't very difficult. If she wasn't doing them perfectly, Frances at least felt her feet were in the general area they were supposed to be.

Fifth position, though, was a killer. One foot had to go behind the other, with the heel of each foot touching the toes of the other foot. The more Frances tried to do it, the more she was sure that, for her feet at least, fifth position was an impossibility. She was relieved when Miss Leticia, standing in front of the room, said, "We seem to be having a little trouble with that one." She laughed a little, and it sounded like bells.

"We'll just have to keep practicing. After we learn our positions and some of the other steps, we'll begin to work on a dance."

A dance! The words shot themselves into Frances's heart. It wouldn't be long now.

The rest of the lesson was spent going over the positions and learning the arm postures that went with them while Mrs. Morton played a song they had learned for assembly once, "Welcome, Sweet

Springtime." Miss Leticia also demonstrated two other steps, plié and relevé, which as near as Frances could tell was squatting down and then rising on tiptoe.

"So"—Miss Leticia smiled at them when the class was finished—"a good beginning, heh?"

Frances wasn't sure whether she should answer out loud or not. There were a few murmurs, but most of the girls just nodded their heads.

"I will see you next week," Miss Leticia said. "Now, practice, practice, practice."

As the girls headed for the dressing room, Polly caught up with Frances. "Practice turning your legs inside out," she whispered.

Even though Frances had liked the lesson, she had to laugh. "I know. I couldn't do fifth position at all."

"Why would you want to?" Polly asked as she went over to her pile of clothes. "It was gross."

Frances started to worry. She wanted Polly to like ballet. "No, it wasn't. Ballet dancers have started this way forever."

"Those that didn't break their legs right at the beginning," Polly retorted. "Hey, Tammi," Polly called over to where Tammi was changing. "I told you the slippers were supposed to be black."

"I'm going to tell Miss Leticia these were the only color they had in my size," she answered huffily. It was plain that Miss Leticia's criticism had stung.

It didn't take Frances long to get dressed. She sat on the bench and waited while Polly threw her leotard into her backpack and pulled her dress over her head.

"So," Frances said as they headed out into the twi-light where Mrs. McAllister was waiting to drive them home, "our first ballet lesson."

"Yeah, there was only one thing wrong with it."

"What's that?" Frances asked.

"It wasn't our last."

5

lizabeth came bounding into the family room on Thursday afternoon. "Tap is wonderful!"

Frances, who had been holding yarn for her grandmother while Grammy wound it into a ball, felt a surge of jealousy go through her. "You danced already?"

Taking a seat next to Grammy on the couch, Elizabeth admitted, "Not exactly. We just learned some steps. But it's going to be great. I can tell."

Grammy beamed at the girls. "My two dancers."

Frances didn't want to disappoint Grammy, but she did say, "Well, not quite yet. But soon."

Elizabeth leaped off the couch. "I'm going to call Ellen. She's taking ballet. And she's going to be jealous we've already learned steps. She just learned positions."

Frances stuck out her tongue at her sister's receding figure. "She knows all I learned was positions, too."

"Patience, patience," Grammy counseled. "And practice. You're going to need a lot of both."

"I know." Frances put down her yarn and moved over to the small space next to her grandmother on the couch. She just fit. "I'm glad you're here."

Grammy looked down at her ankle. "Well, I'm not the most comfortable I've ever been, but at least staying here gives me more time to spend with you. Of course, you're so busy all the time, I'm lucky you have time for me. Tuesday it was ballet, yesterday, basketball."

"Don't remind me," Frances said, and sighed.

When Frances had returned to school on Monday, she had seen Mr. Robinson walking down the halls looking perfectly fit and healthy. Frances knew that meant basketball practice would be starting soon, and sure enough, a notice had gone around that interested parties were to show up on Wednesday. Frances still wasn't very interested, but she had shown up, right behind Polly.

In the gym, as Frances had figured, most of the prospective basketball players were older girls, fifth and sixth graders. She had never felt shorter.

Even Mr. Robinson had looked at her oddly as he started tossing the ball around, just to test their passing and catching skills. "Frances, I'm surprised to see you here."

This had embarrassed Frances horribly, and she shot Polly a dirty look.

Mr. Robinson must have noticed the expression on Frances's face, because he hurriedly added, "Not that we're not happy you're here." He threw the ball to Frances, who promptly dropped it.

At the sound of a few snickers Mr. Robinson frowned. "I don't want to hear that. We're all a team here."

But by the end of the practice, after Frances had dropped a few more passes and thrown wildly whenever it was her turn, even Mr. Robinson looked a little weary. He told several of the girls, including Polly, he was glad that they had signed up for the team. To Frances he merely said good-bye.

Sitting with Grammy's arm around her, it was easy to let the details of the bad practice spill out.

Grammy looked at her. "Why ever do you want to keep going?"

Frances explained about her deal with Polly.

"It doesn't sound like Polly is having a very good time either," Grammy pointed out.

"Well, I don't want her to quit ballet," Frances said stubbornly.

"Why not?"

"We're best friends, and best friends are supposed to do things together. Besides . . ." Frances groped for the words. "It's easier if she's there. Miss Leticia said we were going to have to do steps in front of the class by ourselves. I could never do that if Polly wasn't there."

"Are you sure?" Grammy asked. "Maybe you're underestimating yourself."

Frances shook her head decisively. "No. I need Polly. And if that means I have to go to a few stupid basketball practices, I will."

Grammy looked as if she were going to argue, but instead she picked up her yarn. "Once something gets tangled, it's difficult to untangle," she said.

"I know," Frances replied, even though she wasn't quite sure what Grammy meant. She and Polly weren't tangled up. Everything was fine.

When she talked to Polly on the phone after dinner, she was pleased to hear her friend sounding so excited. But the cause wasn't basketball, and it certainly wasn't ballet. Polly had just spoken to her father.

"I'm going to Milwaukee for part of my Christmas break."

Frances felt a pang of loneliness, but she was so happy for Polly, all she said was, "That's great."

"I'll probably go the day after Christmas. My dad said we might go skiing."

"Well, don't break anything like my grandmother did. You won't be able to go to ballet."

Polly just laughed. "I'm a good skier."

"You are?" This was the first Frances had heard of Polly skiing.

"Sure. My dad and I used to go all the time."

"You're pretty athletic," Frances mused.

"Sure I am."

It was a funny thought. Frances and Bonnie had been so much alike. It was odd to think that now she had a friend who liked so many different things.

"What do you think Mr. Winnow's big surprise is?" Polly asked, changing the subject. Today Mr. Winnow had told his fourth graders that he was going to be giving them some big news as soon as he had the details.

"A party?" Frances suggested.

Polly sighed. "It probably has something to do with an assignment. Mr. Winnow would think doing an oral report is a great surprise."

Other theories were floating around the next day, before class started. Most of the kids had ideas about what the news might be.

"He's probably going to wear a new jacket," Albert said, throwing a wad of paper toward the wastepaper basket at the front of the room and missing. Mr. Winnow had worn the same jacket since school started.

"Maybe we're not going to have math anymore," Tammi suggested from across the aisle.

Frances's heart leaped. Even though Mr. Winnow had been helping her, she still had a hearty dislike for math. Then she realized Tammi's idea was stupid. Teachers just didn't cancel math.

The class didn't have to wait long to find out what Mr. Winnow was so eager to tell them. He leaned against his desk and started speaking almost as soon as the bell rang.

"You probably don't know this," he began, "but before I started teaching here, I was an actor."

A bubble of conversation went around the classroom.

"Did I ever see you on TV?" Sheila asked.

"Yeah, like Mr. Winnow left a great job on television to come here and teach us," Albert snorted.

Mr. Winnow laughed. "I'm afraid Albert's right. I

wasn't a very successful actor, although I did have a few small parts in several plays in Milwaukee."

"Why did you become a teacher?" Polly asked curiously.

"Well, I guess it was because I needed to support myself. And teaching is a little like acting. Only my audience can't get up and leave."

The kids laughed.

"But I do miss the stage," he continued. "When I realized how much, I decided to see if we could put on some kind of production here at the school."

Now the buzzing started again.

"I've left this until the last minute, I know, but I've spoken to most of the teachers and to Mrs. Rotterdam," he said, naming the principal, "and I've got the go-ahead to put on an all-school holiday pageant."

So that was his big news, Frances thought. Well, it did sound like fun.

"Some classes will join together, others will work alone. There will be skits and songs—a little bit of everything. I will supervise the whole production and of course, our own offering. I thought it would be fun to do a skit. I'm writing one now," he said almost shyly.

Tammi raised her hand. "Who's going to have the lead roles?" she wanted to know.

"I thought we'd have tryouts."

"When?" one of the boys asked.

"Monday afternoon. I can tell you this much. The skit is going to be a funny one, and the lead role is Santa Claus. Anybody can bring a piece in on Monday and audition."

It was a little hard to settle down to English after that. Frances wondered if there were any roles for dancers, but she didn't think that she would have the nerve to try out. Even if she did, what would she do? She doubted that anyone would be interested in watching her execute the five ballet positions.

Polly, on the other hand, couldn't wait to try out. On Saturday afternoon she told Frances and Lena about her plans for the audition.

The girls were at Polly's house, sprawled on the floor of her rec room. Frances really liked going over to Polly's. It was quiet and there were no pesky brothers or sisters to bother them.

"I thought I might read a funny poem."

"That would be good," Lena said, grabbing a handful of popcorn from the bowl.

"Or my mom said she could help me find a monologue—that's a speech given by one person—at the library."

"I might try out, but it would be better if I could sing," Lena said, calmly chewing her popcorn.

Frances and Polly looked at her. "Sing?" Frances said. "I didn't know you sing."

"Yes, I do."

"Well, sing something," Polly said, folding her arms.

Without waiting to be asked twice, Lena went right into "Silent Night." It was very pretty.

"You're good," Polly said approvingly.

Frances nodded. "You really are."

"Mr. Winnow didn't say anything about singing parts, so I suppose I'll just read a poem for try-outs."

"He should put in a song just for you," Frances said stoutly.

Lena smiled at her. "I'm going to be singing in my church choir on Christmas Eve, so I'll get to sing anyway."

While Polly and Lena chattered on about the production, Frances looked at them thoughtfully. It was kind of fun to have friends interested in different things. Why had she ever thought that being just like other people was so important?

As much as Frances enjoyed hearing Polly and Lena discuss the audition, she decided that she would pass on it. The thought of getting up in front of the whole class, especially Albert Bell, made her nervous. Dancing was one thing, but acting was something else. Maybe, if she was lucky, there would be a small part for her somewhere in the skit.

"Wait," Polly said. "I have an even better idea for an audition piece."

"What?" Lena wanted to know.

Polly was grinning, but she shook her head. "I don't think I'll tell. I want it to be a surprise."

The girls begged to be let in on the secret, but Polly held firm. "Nope. It'll take a little planning."

On Monday, when the class asked Mr. Winnow if they could start auditioning right away, he smiled and shook his head. "We have a whole day of work to get through, my friends. Then we'll have our auditions."

The day dragged on. English, history, math, lunch, spelling, gym. Finally at two P.M. Mr. Winnow said, "All right, everyone, clear your desks. It's showtime!"

The room came to life. Desks were quickly cleared, and those who had brought something to read took their pages out. Polly raised her hand. "Can I go to the media center?" she asked.

"What for?" Mr. Winnow said, surprised.

"I need to get something. I already arranged it with the librarian."

"Well, go ahead, then. We'll get started without you."

Polly dashed off, while Mr. Winnow grabbed a notebook and headed to the back of the room. "Who would like to go first?"

Several kids raised their hands. Albert Bell waved his so hard, his arm looked as if it were going to fly off. But Mr. Winnow looked past him and pointed to Ralphie Schultz.

Frances wondered what Ralphie was going to do. He was a quiet boy who almost never spoke in class unless called upon. Yet here he was, marching up to the front of the room, a piece of paper clutched in his hand. It turned out to be "The Night Before Christmas."

It wasn't a bad recitation. It wasn't a very good one, either. But when Ralphie got to the line "And visions of sugarplums danced in their heads," Frances began thinking all over again about the Sugar Plum Fairy in *The Nutcracker*. That was the last she heard of Ralphie's poem.

Mr. Winnow had just called on Tammi when Polly came racing back into the room carrying a portable record player with her. Tammi frowned, but Mr. Winnow just motioned Polly to her seat.

Sheila and Leslie dutifully followed Tammi up to the front of the room. "I'm going to sing," Tammi informed everyone. "This is my backup group."

Tammi didn't even try to do anything Christmasy. She sang an oldie called "Stop! In the Name of Love." As near as Frances could tell, all the backup singers did was hum the tune while Tammi sang. They also put their hands up in the air whenever Tammi said "Stop!"

Frances had to admit that Tammi had a pretty fair voice, but she wasn't nearly as good as Lena. Quickly Frances scribbled a note and passed it over. "Lena, you're a million times better!"

Lena just smiled and shrugged.

"Thank you, girls," Mr. Winnow said. "We really don't have any singing roles available, but I guess I can gauge your acting skills from the way you handled the motions."

Frances wasn't sure if he was kidding or not. Tammi didn't seem quite sure either.

A few more kids got up and read monologues. Lena recited a Christmas poem. Then it was Albert's turn. He came up carrying a paper bag.

"I want the part of Santa," he said before he began.

"Oh, do you?" Mr. Winnow said, amused. "Well, let's see what you can do."

"I made up my own poem."

"Fine. Let's hear it."

Albert stuck out his stomach as if he were fat. From the paper bag he took out a Santa's cap. "I didn't have time to find a beard," he said.

"Go ahead, Albert."

" 'How Santa Spends the Summer,' " he began.

"Summer days are long and hot,
My suit feels warm and damp.
So I take it off and head for summer camp.
I'm there with lots of kids,
But I'm kind of old and fat.
It's hard for me to ride or swim
Or swing a baseball bat.
The kids that are nice to me
Will get something good this year.
The others can just go and cry in their beer."

There was surprised applause after Albert finished. Not only was his poem okay, except perhaps that last line, but he had read it with a lot of expression. Miming the action, Albert had even pretended to remove his hot suit, drawing a few whistles from the boys.

Apparently Albert was pleased with his performance as well. He took numerous bows, even after the applause faded away.

"Thank you, Albert," Mr. Winnow said, growing impatient.

"Do I get the part?"

"I haven't made any decisions yet, Albert."

"No one will be better than me," Albert warned.

Mr. Winnow sighed. "I'll let you know. Who's next?"

Polly waved her hand frantically in the air.

"All right, Polly."

It took Polly a few moments to organize herself.

She had to plug in her record player and put on the album she had brought with her. After a few mistries, Polly finally found the right song. Then with a flourish, Polly turned around and began lip-syncing the words to "Santa Claus Is Coming to Town."

Frances watched, amazed, as Polly turned herself into a fat, jolly Santa who was making a list and checking it twice. She didn't even have a hat on her head or stick out her stomach like Albert.

The response to Polly's performance was even more enthusiastic than it had been to Albert's. When Frances glanced in his direction, she could see he was scowling.

Mr. Winnow got up. "I'm certainly gratified by all your efforts. I don't know who is going to get what part yet, but I see we have plenty of talent in this room. We'll continue our auditions tomorrow. One thing's for sure, though." He smiled at them brightly. "This is going to be loads of fun."

The bell rang and the students hurried to gather their things. Frances couldn't wait to tell Polly how good she was, but Albert had gotten there first.

"I suppose you think you've got that Santa part all sewed up, right, broccoli-head?" Albert said.

"Yes, Bell-rhymes-with-smell." Polly calmly stuffed her pencil case into her backpack. "Don't you?"

"Don't count on it."

"Don't bug me." Polly and Albert were eyeball to eyeball. Frances stepped between them.

"Don't you think we should get going?" she asked Polly.

Polly stuck out her tongue, and Albert stuck out his

tongue right back. Then he turned his eyelids inside out and rolled his eyeballs back in his head, one of his favorite tricks.

"Albert, I've never seen you look better," Polly said, stepping around him.

Frances sighed. She had the definite feeling that putting on a skit might not be as much fun as Mr. Winnow hoped.

6

Polly was as nervous as her cat Joey all weekend. By Sunday afternoon, when the girls were at Frances's house playing checkers, Frances had heard Polly say for at least the tenth time, "I wonder who he's picked to play Santa."

"You'll probably find out tomorrow," Frances said for the tenth time. She took advantage of Polly's lack of concentration by jumping her king.

Polly made a face. Then she leaned back on her hands. "You know, if I get that part, I'm going to ask my father to come and see me."

"Do you think he will?" Frances asked with interest.

"Sure." But Polly didn't sound sure.

"You were much better than Albert."

"But Santa Claus is a man," Polly reminded her.

"I remember Mike talking about this Shakespeare play he was reading in English class. He said when the plays were first put on, men played all the women's roles. So why can't you be Santa Claus? With a beard and a red suit, who will know the difference?"

"You're right," Polly said, moving one of her checker pieces. "I just wonder who he picked."

Frances sighed. She hoped Mr. Winnow really would have his decision by tomorrow. She didn't think she could take much more of this.

On Sunday evenings the McAllisters usually ordered pizza for dinner, and whatever the various members of the family were doing—watching the football game on TV or playing or reading—they stopped to eat their pizza and spend a little time together.

Mr. McAllister always said this was a good time to talk about anything that was on their minds. Usually it was nothing major, just discussion about what happened during the week. Frances wanted to talk about her ballet lesson, but Elizabeth was monopolizing the conversation. She had tried out for a role in the holiday pageant. The two sixth-grade classes were joining together for, as Elizabeth's teacher put it, "a cornucopia of Christmas song."

"I really want to be one of the lead singers," Elizabeth said, wiping a bit of cheese off her chin. "And maybe when they find out I can dance, I can do that, too."

Mike looked at his father plaintively. "I don't have to go to this thing, do I, Dad?"

"The show isn't even cast yet," Mr. McAllister murmured.

"That's right," Frances said. She turned to her sister. "And you can't dance yet. You've only had one lesson, just like me."

"I've been practicing," Elizabeth said serenely.

Frances sniffed. So her sister was practicing her three or four steps. Big deal.

"I'm sure you're both taking your dancing very seriously," Grammy said soothingly.

That was another reason Frances liked having Grammy staying with them. Nobody ever ended up fighting when she was around.

Monday came and went without Mr. Winnow saying much about the pageant, other than that he was still working on his skit, trying to write roles for all "his talent," as he put it.

Tuesday he was still working.

Although Frances was anxious to get to ballet class, she waited patiently while Polly went up to Mr. Winnow and asked him if he thought he might be finished with the skit by tomorrow.

"I certainly hope so," he said fervently.

"So you'll give out the parts then."

Mr. Winnow smiled at Polly. "I know it's hard waiting. Remember, as an actor I used to wait to see the cast list go up, too. But I have to make sure that I do right by the pageant. Sometimes a person can have the most talent, but he or she isn't right for the role."

Frances felt her heart drop. Did that mean Mr. Winnow wasn't going to let Polly be Santa Claus because she was a girl?

Polly pulled herself up to her full height. "I think I can play any part. Especially if I can wear a beard."

"I see. Well, let me think about that. I'm not making any promises, though," he warned.

For some reason this conversation seemed to cheer Polly.

"But he practically told you he wasn't going to give you the part," Frances said as they slipped on the newly fallen snow toward Miss Leticia's.

"No," Polly corrected. "He wasn't going to give me the part before I talked to him. Now I think I have a chance."

Polly appeared to be so happy at this turn of events that she didn't even seem to mind putting on her leotard, tights, and slippers. Frances, of course, was excited. This was the moment she had been waiting for all week.

Considering her mood, then, it was a bad shock to walk into the dancing room and see Albert Bell standing at the piano. He was smiling a smile Frances knew well. It said, I'm thinking up ways to cause trouble. Another boy, whom Frances didn't know, was also at the piano, but he was sitting on the bench, running his fingers up and down the keys. Both boys were dressed in T-shirts and shorts. Albert's T-shirt was old and tattered and showed the shark from the movie *Jaws*.

As the girls filtered in, they all looked at Albert and the other boy curiously. But when Polly entered the room, she stood stock still and asked in a loud voice, "What are you doing here?"

Before Albert could answer, Miss Leticia walked into the room with Mrs. Morton right behind her. The pianist scowled at the boy sitting on her bench, and although it took him a few seconds to notice, once he did, he jumped up and moved closer to Albert.

"Bonjour, class," Miss Leticia said.

Everyone mumbled a *bonjour*.

"Have you all been practicing your positions? Good.

We will go over them in a moment. As you may have noticed, we have two new members in class today." She motioned Albert and the other boy to stand next to her. Either she didn't see Albert blowing a bubble with his wad of gum or else she was ignoring it. "This is Albert Bell and Simon Berkey. I'm so pleased we have some boys in the class. When we begin our recital practice, we'll need some gentlemen, *n'est-ce pas?*"

Frances didn't know what "ness pah" meant, but she was positive a "gentleman" wouldn't, at this moment, be crossing his eyes and wrinkling his nose at the rest of the class as if he smelled something bad.

"We'll line up now, as we did last week, by height."

As the students shuffled into line. Frances watched to see where Albert wound up. He was a little shorter than Polly, so he stood in front of her.

Miss Leticia nodded at Mrs. Morton, who began with a slow, swaying sort of song while they learned a few warmup exercises. Next came the five positions. Frances was just trying to shape her feet into that difficult fifth position when she heard a squeal from the end of the line.

"She's stepping on me!" Albert said indignantly. "Aunt Leticia, I mean Miss Leticia, Polly Brock stepped on me."

"I did not."

"Did too."

"Children, please!" Miss Leticia clapped her hands together.

"Did not," Frances could hear Polly mutter.

After what seemed like a very long time on the

positions, Miss Leticia taught the class to arabesque, which meant standing on one leg while extending the other out behind. This apparently gave Albert an idea, because after Miss Leticia called out arabesque, Polly squealed, "Get your toe out of my stomach!"

Miss Leticia looked as if she were getting a headache. The class continued practicing their steps until she announced, "Now I want to try something a little different."

Good, Frances thought. She still loved ballet, but even she had to admit this was getting tiresome.

"In the next few months I'd like to have some sort of a program for your friends and family so they can see how you're progressing. We won't actually do a ballet, of course, because you won't be ready for that by then. But I thought we could put on a display of movement with a bit of a story to it."

That sounded close enough to a ballet for Frances. She leaned closely to hear what Miss Leticia was going to say next.

"We will use a story I've done before with other beginning classes. It is the story of a boy and girl who go out in the forest. They lose their way and are helped by various animals in the woods, who assist them in finding food and shelter. They are almost hurt by a hunter, but the animals help them escape."

Frances could already see herself in the role of the little girl. She would wear a dress with a short skirt and a crisp white blouse—like Heidi wore. Then she had an awful thought. What if Albert was the boy? She certainly didn't want to get lost in the woods with him. Maybe it was time to look over Simon more closely. Discreetly she glanced over her shoulder. Simon was wiping his glasses on his shirt. He had a thin little face to match his thin body. His blond hair, which was thin as well, lay plastered back on his head. Frances didn't think she would want to get lost in the woods with him either.

She tried to picture herself on the stage without either Albert or Simon, but then she had another thought. Could she actually get up on the stage in a solo part? She certainly didn't want to stand out in the holiday pageant the way Polly did. Maybe she would prefer to be one of the animals, so she could be onstage with them. Frances sighed. On the one hand, all she wanted to do was dance. On the other, she didn't know if she would ever have the nerve to perform in front of people. Why did this have to be so complicated?

Frances didn't want to think any more about this dilemma. She turned her attention back to Miss Leticia, who was saying, "So why don't we begin by acting out some of the motions little animals might make. How about rabbits? How do they move?"

Miss Leticia started hopping around the room. Soon all the kids were hopping, embarrassedly at first, then with more vigor. Frances hadn't hopped around like this since she was in kindergarten, but it was sort of fun. Even Polly wore a smile and bounced around the room.

Albert's expression, however, was far from happy as he jumped about the room. He looked determined, like a man with a mission. That mission seemed to be bouncing as high as he could, then trying to land as near people's toes as possible. Soon the exercise became a frantic effort to stay away from Albert.

Miss Leticia, who was bouncing with her back to Albert, didn't notice the nervous bunnies behind her. When she turned around, Albert quickly screeched to a halt and pasted an angelic smile on his face.

"Now let's be birds," Miss Leticia said.

Being a bird was the perfect opportunity for Albert to spread his wings and start zooming around the room. He looked more like an airplane than a bird, and he tried to engage Simon in a battle, but Simon flew away from him. Frances was pleased to see that Simon seemed to be taking his ballet a lot more seriously than Albert did.

Each time Miss Leticia changed animals Albert was able to turn it to his own advantage. Everyone tried to ignore him until, as a squirrel, he pretended to nibble at Polly's leg. Pulling it away from him, she said in a loud voice, "Miss Leticia, Albert Bell is bothering me. Again."

"He is?" Miss Leticia turned around in surprise.

"Yes. And he's bugging everyone else, too."

Frances looked in awe at Polly. Tattling on Albert to his own aunt! She would never have had the nerve.

"Is this true, class?" At their nods Miss Leticia frowned. "Albert, I will have a word with you after class. Now let's do some cool-down exercises before dismissal."

Cool-downs were nice, relaxing exercises, but

Frances wasn't very relaxed while she did them. She couldn't wait for class to be over, so she could find out what was going to happen to Albert.

Polly had the same idea, because the moment Miss Leticia said *"Au revoir,"* Polly ran over to Frances and whispered, "Let's go into the ladies' room. If we open the door a crack, we can hear what they're saying."

So while the rest of the class moved into the changing room, Polly and Frances ducked into the washroom, which was right next to Miss Leticia's office. With the door slightly open they could hear everything.

"Albert, I thought we had a deal," Miss Leticia said with a sigh. "You were going to attend classes and not cause trouble, and I was going to buy you that bike you wanted for Christmas." Miss Leticia's voice did not have that lovely lilting sound now.

"I wasn't causing trouble. Not really."

"You were being disruptive."

"Oh, that's what fat old Polly Brock says."

Polly quivered indignantly. "I'm not fat!"

"Albert. Do we have a deal or not? I have to have a few boys in the class, and you know your mother said she was signing you up, no matter what. This way you get a bike out of the deal. But in any case, you have to come to lessons."

"Aww . . ."

"It's up to you, Albert."

The girls had heard enough. They sneaked out of the bathroom and into the changing room. Most of the students were already dressed and ready to go, so by the time Frances and Polly finished changing, they were alone.

"Boy," Frances said as she buttoned her blouse, "Miss Leticia should have bribed some other boy to come take ballet lessons. Albert's no bargain at any price."

"That's for sure," Polly said with disgust. "Ballet is bad enough, but with Albert Bell here . . ." Her voice trailed off.

"Do you really hate it that much?" Frances asked. "I thought maybe you were starting to like it better."

"Nope," Polly said bluntly. "I especially didn't like jumping around like the world's biggest Easter bunny."

Frances felt bad, but all she said was, "Well, I'm awfully glad you were here. No one else would have had the guts to tell on Albert. I know I wouldn't have."

Polly pulled on her coat, and they walked outside. "No big deal. With people like Albert, you just have to show them who's boss."

"Awwght!" Albert Bell came flying out of the dance studio right behind them and landed with a thump in front of the girls.

"Albert, are you crazy?" Polly cried. "You almost gave us a heart attack!"

"Now I'm showing *you* who's boss," he said, smirking.

"You were listening," Frances said accusingly.

"Like you weren't when my aunt was talking to me?"

The girls didn't have an answer for that.

Albert began talking in a gangster's voice. "Now listen up. I don't want you causing me any more trouble. Either of you."

Frances felt a little tremble when he turned his gaze on her, but Polly just stood up a bit straighter. "If you don't cause trouble, we won't either."

"I really want that bike. And I'm going to get it."

"Fine. So just be a good little ballet dancer." Polly smirked. "Gee, I wonder what the guys in class are going to say when they hear you're a Mr. Twinkle Toes."

"Oh, I already told 'em, because I knew one of you would try that. I just said my aunt is bribing me, and it's a great deal."

Trust Albert to have an angle already figured out, Frances thought.

"Now, I don't want you messing anything up for me," he continued.

Polly shrugged. "That's entirely up to you, Albert Bell. Come on," she said, pulling Frances by the arm. "We'll leave Albert here. He might have a few new steps he wants to learn. He's going to be nice and leave all the girls alone, or he's never going to get that bike. Right, Al?"

Albert's face turned as red as his hair. "You're going to be sorry, Brock."

"Not me. All I have to do is tell Miss Leticia you're bothering me . . ." She didn't have to finish the sentence. Albert stalked off.

"Gee, you made him mad."

Polly shrugged. "Who cares? Wait until I get the role of Santa Claus. He's really going to be angry then."

frances saw the basketball coming toward her. She knew she should reach out her hands and grab for it, but instead she stepped out of the way, allowing it to bounce forlornly down the side of the gym. Mr. Robinson blew his whistle. He was losing patience with Frances. She always seemed to do just the opposite of what she was supposed to on the basketball court.

"Frances, when one of your team members passes you the ball, that usually means they would like you to catch it."

"I know," Frances mumbled.

Mr. Robinson shook his head. "Next time, try to accommodate them. All right, girls. Practice dismissed."

Several of the older girls gave Frances withering glances as they walked past her to the locker room. Polly was more direct. "Frances, you stink."

"Well, if it wasn't for you, I wouldn't be here at all," she replied indignantly.

"No," Polly corrected, "if it wasn't for you. You only got involved in this so I would come to ballet."

There was no way to deny that. It was the truth. Frances still wanted the security of Polly at Miss Leticia's, but she sure wished there was some way out of these humiliating basketball sessions.

Frances tried to make herself invisible while she changed her clothes. She didn't want any of the other girls to feel they had to make remarks about her playing.

Polly, however, chattered away. She was in a good mood. Mr. Winnow had announced the parts for the skit that afternoon.

"It was a very hard decision," he said, sitting at his desk holding a piece of paper in his hands. "There are parts for everyone, but not leading roles, of course. Because I had so many good contenders, I had to change the skit quite a lot. It's about two Santas now. One's real, one's an impostor. The real Santa is getting ready for Christmas, but the fake wants to be the one to ride in the sleigh and deliver the presents. He tries all kinds of tricks to get rid of Santa, and he finally succeeds by taking a part off the sleigh, so that Santa has to go off and find a new one. Fortunately an elf named Tiger realizes what's happened and finds Santa just in time for Christmas Eve. Santa realizes that the fake only wanted to experience Christmas in a special way, so he lets him ride along. That's why the title of the skit is *The Two-Santa Christmas*."

Frances doodled on a piece of paper as Mr. Winnow read off the names of the cast. Lena was Mrs. Claus,

Tammi was Tiger, and Albert and Polly were the Santas—Polly was the real one and Albert the fake.

Polly was elated with her role. As the girls walked home together after basketball practice, Polly told Frances how she planned to learn all her lines quickly, so that she could be the first person to work without a script.

"And I'm going to call my father after supper and ask him if he'll come," Polly said excitedly.

"Do you think he will?"

"Of course," Polly said confidently. "He wouldn't miss my debut."

Frances hoped Polly was right.

Polly wasn't the only one who had grabbed an important role in the pageant. Elizabeth was on the phone when Frances got home, telling a friend who had been home sick that day that she was going to sing a solo, "The First Noel."

Frances wandered forlornly into the guest room where Grammy was sitting on the leather chair, her feet up on the ottoman. She used the remote control to turn down the volume on the television when Frances walked into the room.

"What's wrong, hon? You look as if you just lost your best friend."

Frances sat down on the bed. "I did. Kind of."

"Is something wrong with Polly?"

"No. But she got one of the leads in the skit for our holiday pageant."

"Well, that's good, isn't it?"

"And Elizabeth is going to be singing a solo."

"What about you?"

"I didn't want any special parts."

Grammy frowned. "I don't understand. What's the problem then?"

"I don't know. It just seems like everyone is going to be working on the pageant. No one else is afraid to be onstage," Frances burst out.

"So that's it," Grammy said, nodding. "You're feeling like you can't get past your fears."

Frances leaned back on the bed. "Whenever I think about dancing in front of people, I get all excited. But if I actually had to do it, well, I'm not sure that I could."

"People never know what they can do until they try."

"But I don't want to try."

Grammy gave a slight shrug. "Then you're going to have to live with that choice."

Frances thought about that. "It's like basketball, you mean."

"I'm afraid I'm not following you."

"Well, I'm going to basketball, and I'm terrible at that. I hate the way the girls look at me, but at least it keeps Polly coming to ballet lessons."

Studying Frances carefully, Grammy finally nodded. "We all make choices about what we're going to do in this life. You found out you're not very good in basketball, but you're going to keep going because you get something out of it. Maybe if you took a part in the pageant, you'd get something out of that as well."

"It's too late for that," Frances said. "The parts have

all been assigned. Besides, it's one thing to make a fool of yourself in front of some girls trying out for the basketball team. Goofing up in front of a whole auditorium full of people is something else."

"When you think it's worth it, Frances, you'll try to do something that's hard for you."

Lying on her bed in her room later, Frances wondered if Grammy was right. When the time came, would she be brave enough to get up and dance in a recital? She hoped so. In the meantime, she supposed that all she could do was be happy for Polly, and even Elizabeth. After all, they were just doing what they wanted to.

The next day was the first rehearsal, and the school had a bad case of pageant fever. Each room was assigned a time period when they would rehearse. Mr. Winnow's fourth graders had the assembly hall the hour before lunch.

The first grade was just finishing up when Frances's class tiptoed in. Mr. Winnow put his finger to his lips as the kids took their seats and watched the little ones singing "Jingle Bells."

They were so cute, Frances thought. Thin, happy little voices spread out over the assembly hall. Many of the first graders didn't seem to realize they were standing onstage singing in front of older kids. They acted just like always, shifting from foot to foot and poking one another every once in a while.

After they had trundled offstage and out of the assembly hall, Mr. Winnow brought his fourth graders forward. "Those in the first scene, take your places." he said. "The rest of you can wait backstage. You're going to have to learn how to be quiet back there, because if you're noisy, the audience can hear you. I'll be sitting in the front row."

Most of the kids who hadn't gotten major roles were Santa's elves. Frances was glad to be an elf. The other alternative was to be a reindeer and wear a fuzzy brown costume with antlers. She wanted no part of that.

Polly, of course, was onstage right at the beginning, as was Lena. Frances decided to sit in one corner of the stage and watch them until she came out with the rest of the second stringers.

She was just settling in, watching Polly and Lena as Mr. and Mrs. Santa have a cup of hot chocolate, when she heard a commotion behind her. Turning to look, she saw Albert Bell putting on a papier-mâché duck head. It must have been left over from some other class play.

A couple of the boys started laughing. "Hey, Bell, I bet you a dollar you won't go out there wearing that thing."

"Make it five," Albert's muffled voice replied.

"No way," Robert Melton said. "You probably don't even have five dollars."

"Then I'm taking it off."

"Chicken!"

"You mean, duck," one of the other guys said, and laughed.

"Albert, your cue is coming up," hissed Susie Won, who had been designated the stage manager.

"Okay, okay." Albert tried to pull the duck head off, but it seemed stuck.

"Albert, two more lines and then you're on," Susie insisted. "Take that thing off!"

"I can't." Albert's muffled voice sounded frantic.

Frances could hear Polly saying the line that was to bring Albert onstage. Unfortunately it was, "Look, dear, here comes a fellow who looks just like me!"

Albert stumbled onstage, and Frances watched Polly's eyes grow wide. "You're doing that on purpose!" she yelled.

"No, I'm not!"

Kids, teachers, anyone within sight of Albert started laughing.

"Albert, what's going on?" Mr. Winnow bounded up from his seat.

"This thing got stuck on my head."

"Oh, Albert." Mr. Winnow, walking as though the weight of the world were on his shoulders, climbed onstage. He sat Albert down and, twisting and turning carefully, managed to extricate Albert from the duck head.

While Mr. Winnow was giving Albert a lecture on his responsibilities as a leading actor, Polly stalked over to Frances. "Did you see that?"

"I think we all saw it, Polly."

"I bet he did that just to throw me."

"I don't think so. It was just a typical Albert Bell move."

Polly crossed her arms. "Well, he better not screw up on the night of the performance. Not with my father in the audience."

"He's coming, then?"

"Yep. He said he'd have to check his schedule,

but I'm pretty sure that means he's going to come. I told him I had the leading role."

Frances didn't like the sound of "checking his schedule," but maybe it would all work out. "I'm sure he'll enjoy it," she told Polly.

"Yeah," Polly said, looking over at Albert. "As long as Albert remembers to say 'Ho, ho, ho' instead of 'Quack, quack, quack.'"

By Saturday, Frances's new attitude about the pageant—live and let live—was wearing a little thin. She and Polly were supposed to go to the movies that afternoon, but Polly insisted on staying home and studying her lines. Frances played all the other parts, repeating the lines again and again until she almost had them memorized.

"We could still catch the second show," Frances said, looking at her watch.

Polly got up, stretched, and walked around her TV room. "Not today, Frances. I'm still messing up the lines in the second act. Gee, I'm stiff." She rubbed her arms.

"You've practically been sitting in one position all day long. That's why you're all cramped."

With exaggerated care, Polly did a few pliés. "There, now, I've gotten my exercise and practiced my ballet, too."

Frances didn't want to tell Polly that she really did practice her positions and steps every night, no matter how boring they got sometimes, so all she said was, "Good. Then we can go to the movies."

Before Polly could do more than shake her head,

the phone rang. "Daddy," she said when she answered it, a big smile on her face. "How are you?"

But the smile quickly faded as the conversation progressed. "You can't?" Polly said, her voice dripping with disappointment. "Oh, I know you would . . . No, it's okay. No . . . I love you, too, Daddy. Okay, bye."

Frances didn't have to hear Mr. Brock's end of the conversation to know what he said. She only had to look at Polly, who was trying hard not to cry.

"I'm sorry," Frances said sympathetically.

But Polly didn't want Frances's comfort. "He's very busy. He's got companies to run. It's not like he just owns a hardware store or something."

Frances felt as if she had been slapped. She stood up, grabbed her coat, and headed for the door. "Well, at least my father is always around when I need him," she told Polly shakily before she left.

Frances thought she'd feel better after she said this, but as she walked home through the crunchy snow, she only felt worse.

8

"But Grammy, she shouldn't have said that about Dad."

Frances was curled up next to her grandmother on the couch in the television room. She sometimes spent Saturday night sleeping over at Polly's house, or vice versa, but there was no question of doing that tonight. Things had been as icy as the air outside when Frances had left the Brocks'.

Grammy pulled Frances close. "No, she shouldn't, but she must have been awfully upset."

Frances nodded. "She was almost crying."

"I bet she's sorry she was so rude. Probably doesn't know how to apologize either."

"Polly's not too good at apologizing," Frances agreed.

"Maybe you should make the first move."

"Me!"

"It wouldn't hurt," Grammy said blandly. "You can afford to be big when you know you're right."

Frances mulled this over. She knew that Polly liked

Mr. McAllister. They were always laughing together when she came over to the house. The more Frances thought about it, the surer she became that if Polly hadn't been so upset, she never would have said what she did. "I guess I could call her," Frances finally said.

"Why don't you do it now," Grammy encouraged her.

"All right." Frances got up and went to the phone in the kitchen. Her parents had gone bowling, and Elizabeth and Mike were out, so at least she would have a little privacy.

"Polly, it's Frances," she said as soon as Polly answered.

"Hi," Polly replied softly.

"Ah, about this afternoon . . ."

"Oh, Frances, I'm so glad you called. I was a rat for saying mean things about your dad."

"Not a rat. A mouse, maybe." Both girls giggled.

"I just felt so bad about . . . well, you know," Polly continued.

"I know."

"He'd be there if he could. He's just so busy." But Polly didn't really sound convinced.

"Maybe his plans will change, and he'll be able to make it."

"I'm not going to count on that."

"You never know."

After Frances hung up, she leaned against the refrigerator twirling the phone cord. The more she thought about it, the angrier she got. How could Mr. Brock keep disappointing Polly like that? If there was only some way she could make Mr. Brock change his plans. But there probably wasn't much chance of that.

Frances thought about Polly and her father the rest of the evening. She even dreamed about them. In her dream Polly was at a train station waiting for her father to come and see her off, but he never showed up. It woke Frances up, and she lay in bed thinking about the sad look on Polly's face in the dream.

She wanted to go over to Polly's the next day, but at breakfast her mother had some news. "Aunt Nan and Uncle Otto and the kids are coming over," she said brightly. "They want to see how Grammy is doing."

"They're not bringing that dog, are they?" Mr. McAllister wanted to know.

"Oh, I doubt that," Grammy said dryly.

"I think I have to study at the library," Mike said, helping himself to some waffles.

"You can go for an hour, then I want you back here," his mother said tartly.

"Yeah, we're not going to entertain Sissy and Roy all by ourselves," Elizabeth informed him.

"What do you expect *me* to do? Play with Roy? He's just a little kid."

"But twice as smart as you." Elizabeth said, and laughed.

"All right, all right, that's it," Mrs. McAllister said. "I've got a lot to do this afternoon. I don't want any arguing."

"What are you making for dinner?" Frances asked.

"Turkey. I figure I owe everyone one." She smiled

when she saw the horrified looks on Frances's and Elizabeth's faces. "But don't worry. I'm not going the whole pie and mashed potatoes route. I can handle this dinner myself."

That didn't mean that Frances and Elizabeth weren't pressed into cleanup duty.

"I don't see why I have to do the bathroom," Frances complained later as she took the cleaning supplies out of the broom closet. "All Elizabeth's doing is making her bed. Just because my side of the room is neat, I shouldn't be punished."

"Frances, I appreciate the fact that you keep your things neat, but that doesn't mean you don't have to do your part."

"I do my part and everyone else's," Frances muttered. She trudged upstairs. As usual, Elizabeth was singing "The First Noel." It used to be one of Frances's favorite carols, but now she was beginning to hate it. Elizabeth caroled it at all hours of the day and night. Frances had even heard Elizabeth humming it in her sleep.

"You're going to wear your voice out," Frances warned.

"In fields where they lay . . ." Elizabeth boomed.

"Fine. But you'll be sorry on the day of the pageant when you have a sore throat."

Elizabeth stopped making her bed and came into the bathroom where Frances was scouring away.

"Do you think Mr. Winnow is going to direct me?"

Frances knew that Elizabeth had a major crush on Mr. Winnow. No matter how much she liked to tease her sister, she didn't feel right teasing her about this. "What do you mean, direct you?"

"Well, he is in charge of putting the whole pageant together. He might want to coach me privately. Help me with my hand motions or something."

Frances shook her head pityingly. "I don't think so. He's awfully busy."

"But he might," Elizabeth insisted.

"Anything's possible," Frances answered, but thought to herself, Boy, I hope I never do anything dopey like get a crush on a teacher.

This time the turkey was roasting in the oven when the Ritz family arrived. Sammy was nowhere in sight.

"Mother, how are you?" Aunt Nan cried. She ran over to Grammy, who was stretched out on the couch, and gave her a hug and a big kiss. Aunt Nan could be very dramatic.

After she had kissed her grandmother, Sissy came over to Elizabeth and Frances. "So what are we going to do?"

Elizabeth looked at her distastefully. "What do you want to do?"

"Why don't we write letters to movie stars?"

"Why would we do that?" Frances asked, puzzled.

"So they'll answer back," Sissy said impatiently. She dug into her bag and drew out a book. The cover was red with yellow stars all over it. *Star Directory,* it read.

Elizabeth took the book out of Sissy's hand. "Hey, this is neat," she exclaimed. "Here's the address of that cute guy on *Fun House.*"

Frances was unimpressed. She certainly didn't want to spend the afternoon writing to people on television. Turning to Roy, she asked, "What do you want to do? We still don't have Trival Pursuit," she hastened to add.

"Do you have any cookbooks?" Roy asked.

"What for?"

"I'm thinking of becoming a chef when I grow up."

Great, Frances thought with disgust. I can spend the afternoon watching Sissy and Elizabeth write letters, or I can find out how to fry chicken. She went into the television room where Mike was sitting with Mr. McAllister and Uncle Otto watching a football game. Mike was busily cheering the Green Bay Packers when Frances accidentally walked in front of the television.

"Hey, short stuff, get out of the way," he bellowed.

"Well, excuse me." Frances took a seat next to Uncle Otto on the couch.

"Like football?" he asked conversationally.

"Not really."

"Then why are you watching?"

Frances couldn't very well say, Because your daughter's silly and your son's weird. "Nothing else to do."

Mr. McAllister looked at her and frowned. "Frances, there are lots of interesting things you could be doing."

Tell that to the other kids, Frances wanted to say.

"Now, I know you're no football fan. Why don't you find your cousins and go play with them," her father continued.

Boy, she couldn't even watch television in her own television room, Frances thought. Trying to maintain a little dignity, she got up and left. Someone was making a touchdown, so nobody really noticed she was going.

She wandered into the kitchen where her mother, Grammy, and Aunt Nan were having a cup of coffee. Roy was sitting on the floor reading, his legs crossed Indian style. Apparently he had found his cookbook.

"So what's for supper," Frances joked halfheartedly, sitting down next to him.

"Quiche." Roy barely looked up.

"What's that?"

Roy gave her a pitying glance. "It's a French dish. An egg custard filled with cheese and other ingredients, like bacon."

"Why don't you just make bacon and eggs?"

"Oh, Frances." Roy heaved a sigh, as though Frances were a burden he had to bear. "Anybody could make bacon and eggs."

In point of fact, Frances couldn't. Not very well, anyway. "C'mon, Roy. Let's do something else. How about a game of checkers?"

"I haven't played checkers since I was four. What about chess?"

"I don't know how to play chess," Frances replied, though it galled her to admit it.

"I think I'd rather look through the cookbooks then. Your mother has some very interesting ones."

Frances got up. "Fine. *Bon appétit.*" She was glad she could throw out this French phrase, which she had heard a lady chef on television say.

There was nothing left to do but go upstairs and see what Elizabeth and Sissy were up to. Maybe by now they had given up the idea of writing letters to people who'd never write back and were ready to have some fun. But when she walked into her bedroom, the girls were hard at work. Each had a sheet of Elizabeth's fancy stationery, and they were scribbling away.

"So which lucky stars are going to be your pen pals?" she asked sarcastically.

Elizabeth barely looked up. "I'm writing to the lead singer of the Charley Boys."

"The guy on *Fun House*," Sissy mumbled.

"What makes you think they'll answer?"

"Well, they might not," Sissy said. "But maybe we'll get an autographed picture or something."

"On the other hand, maybe they will write back." Elizabeth looked down at the letter dreamily. "They'll get our letters and think, What smart, intelligent girls. And maybe they'll even want to meet us."

"Right. Then they're probably going to want to marry you. That would be the next logical step."

"Oh, Frances, where's your sense of adventure? It can't hurt to write. Who knows what will happen?"

Frances spent the rest of the afternoon on her bed reading. It was hard to concentrate between Elizabeth's and Sissy's giggles and whispers. She wondered what had happened to Elizabeth's dislike for Sissy. They seemed like best friends at the moment.

Finally Mrs. McAllister called everyone to dinner. Even without the mashed potatoes and fancy side dishes, it was still a pretty festive meal. Frances finally relaxed and enjoyed herself while Uncle Otto entertained everyone with stories of his days as a minor league baseball player.

All through dinner, however, Frances kept trying to think of something. There was an elusive thought floating around in her brain, but she couldn't quite put her finger on it. Finally during dessert it came to her. Letter writing. Maybe there was a way that a letter could help Polly.

After the Ritzes had left, with the same wild flurry of hugs and kisses that they had entered with, Frances's germ of an idea began to flourish. What if she wrote Mr. Brock a letter? She could tell him how much Polly wanted him to come to the holiday pageant. Maybe if he realized how important his presence was to Polly, he'd cancel his business plans and be there the way his daughter needed him to be.

Grammy was in her room getting ready for bed when Frances approached her with the idea. "What do you think?" she asked her grandmother once she explained her plan.

"Well." Grammy put down her toothpaste and gave Frances her full attention. "I guess that depends on what Polly would think of it."

"I don't want to tell Polly," Frances said firmly. "She'd tell me not to get involved."

"Then maybe you shouldn't."

Frances was stubborn. "Nope. If her dad does come, she'll be really happy. And if he doesn't, I never have to tell her I wrote."

"Sounds like you thought this one out."

"I have. And isn't it a good idea?"

Grammy slipped off her robe and used her cane to get to the bed. "Turn down the cover for me, will you, hon?"

"Sure." Frances dutifully took off the bedspread and put it on a chair. "Don't you think this could work out great, Grammy?"

"Might. Might not." Grammy looked at Frances with a smile on her face. "But I guess it's worth trying."

Frances soon found out, however, that having an idea and carrying it out were two different things. For starters, she didn't have Mr. Brock's address, and she didn't want to ask Polly for it.

In desperation she went to the library after school on Monday. Carefully avoiding Mrs. Brock, who was sitting at the reference desk, she located the Milwaukee phone book. There were so many Brocks it was impossible to tell which one was Polly's father.

It took a bit of persuading, but Frances convinced her mother that she needed to study at Polly's house that evening. Polly was a little surprised to see her, but glad, of course.

Frances felt a little guilty about deceiving Polly, but she told herself it was for Polly's own good. When Polly went to the bathroom, Frances sneaked a look at Polly's address book, which she knew her friend kept in the top drawer of her desk. Sure enough, there was Mr. Brock's address, which Frances quickly copied down on a scrap of paper and stuffed into her pocket.

"What are you doing over there?" Polly asked quizzically, coming into the room.

"Nothing."

"You look so funny."

Fortunately Frances had put the book away, so there was no evidence of what she had been up to. "I'm just checking out your . . . pen," she said, picking one up from the desk.

"Why?" There's nothing special about it."

"Oh, I have one just like it."

Polly shrugged. "Who doesn't?" But at least she didn't think any more of it, and the girls started their homework.

Frances couldn't wait to get home to write her letter. She let Polly help her with her math, and then she called her mother for a ride home.

After taking off her coat and hanging it up, Frances dashed upstairs to write her letter. Chewing on her pencil, Frances tried to get clear in her mind just what she wanted to say. Finally she wrote:

Dear Mr. Brock,
You don't know me, but I'm your daughter Polly's friend. She misses you very much. It's very hard for her when you cancel your plans. Polly has one of the leads in the holiday pageant. I know you are very busy, but I hope you will come to see her. It would mean a lot to Polly. Thank you.

Sincerely,
Frances McAllister
(414) 555-3546

P.S. Polly doesn't know I wrote this letter.

Frances stuffed the letter into an envelope and licked the stamp. There, she thought. She had done what she could. Now it was Mr. Brock's turn.

9

" Frances, I have to talk to you." Polly looked uneasy.

"Okay."

The girls were looking for a table in the lunchroom. Lena was absent today, so when they found two seats they grabbed them.

"What's up?" Frances asked. She had seen Polly in many moods, but nervous was usually not one of them.

"I don't want to go to ballet today."

"Aren't you feeling well?" Frances's tone was concerned.

"No. I'm all right."

"But we're going to practice our story dance today."

Polly stirred her spaghetti absently. "I know."

"So?"

"I want to go home and study my lines for the skit."

"Oh, Polly, you already know them by heart."

"Well, that's not exactly all of it." Polly paused. "I hate ballet, Frances."

Frances was shocked. She wasn't stupid. She'd known that Polly didn't like ballet much. But hate it? That was an awfully strong word.

"I don't want to go anymore at all."

"But you promised," Frances wailed.

"I know, I know. It's such a waste of time, though. Especially now, when I really want to spend my free time rehearsing my lines. Can't you understand that?"

Frances stared down at her plate. She knew that she should tell Polly to forget ballet if she disliked it so much, but she didn't know if she could face going to the lessons alone.

"All right," Polly snapped, not waiting for an answer. "I'll go if it means so much to you."

Frances didn't know what to say but "Thanks."

All afternoon, though, she had an uneasy feeling in her stomach. She thought about how much she disliked basketball. What if she had told Polly she wanted to quit, and Polly wouldn't let her. That would be terrible. When the last bell rang, Frances walked over to Polly's locker.

"Are you ready?" Polly asked in the same cool tone she had used throughout the rest of their lunch.

"You don't have to go with me."

"What?" Polly asked in surprise.

"I shouldn't make you come with me when you want to concentrate on learning your lines."

"Well, thanks," Polly said softly. "I could go, though . . . . I can run through my lines later."

Frances was very tempted to take Polly up on her

offer. She had done her part by giving Polly a way out. If Polly still wanted to go to Miss Leticia's . . . But Frances steeled herself against that line of thinking. It was plain that Polly was only trying to be a good friend. The least Frances could do was be a good friend too.

"No. That's okay."

It was a lonely walk to Miss Leticia's. Frances could have joined some of the other girls headed in the same direction, but she was too shy to do that. So she shuffled along in the snow, hoping that perhaps Albert Bell had decided that he wanted to stay home and go over his lines, too.

Unfortunately the first person that Frances saw when she walked through the door was Albert sitting on the piano bench picking out "Chopsticks."

"Hi, McShrimp," he said, looking up.

Frances decided to just walk by, but Albert jumped up and stood in front of her. "Where's the Big Mac?"

"If you're speaking of Polly, she's home practicing for the skit," Frances said stiffly. "Maybe you ought to be doing the same."

"Not me. I know my lines." He began spouting off a couple of them to prove it.

Frances walked past him into the dressing room and said hello to a couple of the girls. She was just in the midst of undressing when she saw the curtain that separated the changing room from the dance area move just a little. Tammi noticed it too.

"Hey, what's that?" she hissed.

Frances looked more closely. Was that an eye and

a bit of a nose visible in the crack? "Do you see what I do?" Frances asked.

Tammi marched over to the curtain and pulled it aside, but there was no one there. Frances glimpsed Albert, who was at the piano looking positively angelic.

"He's going to get it someday," Tammi muttered.

Frances wished she'd be the one to give it to him, but that was unlikely.

Dance class began as it always did, with Miss Leticia taking attendance. There were a couple of kids missing, including Simon. When Polly's name was called, Frances thought it was her duty to say something. "She couldn't be here today," Frances said softly.

"She'll catch up," Miss Leticia replied with a smile.

Frances couldn't bear to tell the dance teacher the class might have seen the last of Polly.

Then it was time for warmup exercises and positions. A few new steps were added for good measure.

Frances's legs were just starting to ache a little when Miss Leticia clapped her hands. "Why don't we practice our story dance now, children?"

Frances wondered if it was time to start hopping like a bunny again. But Miss Leticia had another idea.

"I'm going to try some of you out for the individual roles."

Oh, no, Frances thought. She didn't want to get out on the floor all by herself, especially if Polly wasn't there.

"Let's see, now." Miss Leticia called out the names of several girls to play animals. Then she said, "And for the girl, how about Frances. Albert, you can be the boy."

Could this be happening? If there was anything worse than dancing alone, it was dancing with Albert.

"Come, come." Miss Leticia positioned the animals out on the floor. "Now, Albert and Frances, I want you to enter stage left, holding hands."

Frances's horrified look was met by one of Albert's own. Mrs. Morton began tinkling a tune on the piano, but Albert and Frances just stood there, as if rooted to the spot.

"What are you waiting for?" Miss Leticia asked.

Frances couldn't tell her she was waiting for the floor to open up and swallow her.

"Well, let's do it," Albert said gruffly. He grabbed her hand and dragged her out on the floor.

Miss Leticia frowned. "Albert, a little more gracefully, please. Now, both of you, walk around a bit as though you are admiring the trees and the flowers. It's a beautiful day, a perfect day to be out in the forest. Please begin."

It took every ounce of imagination Frances had to pretend she was wandering through a lovely pastoral scene on a warm day while Albert Bell was gripping her hand as if he were about to break it off, but she managed.

"Good, Frances, but Albert, you're staring at the floor. Look around you, please."

Frances stole a peek at Albert, whose idea of glancing around the forest was staring at the ceiling instead of the floor. He didn't look cocky, as he usually did. He just looked embarrassed.

"Now, children, start picking the flowers."

At least this bit of instruction gave Frances the opportunity to remove her hand from Albert's, which was beginning to sweat. She pretended to pick a few flowers. She even held one up to her nose and sniffed it.

"Rabbit," Miss Leticia directed, "hop in front of the children."

Terry, the girl who was playing Rabbit, was the tallest girl in the class. She didn't make a very graceful bunny.

"Albert, pat her head."

"Now, wait a minute," Albert objected.

"Albert . . ." his aunt said warningly.

Albert gave the rabbit a few bops on the head, though he had to reach up to do it. Frances suppressed her giggles.

"Frances, now you notice the animals. Go over to each of them and greet them—touch them or whisper hello."

Doing as she was told, Frances tried to be as graceful in her movements as Albert was awkward. She glided over to the bird and gave it a gentle pat. Say, this is kind of fun, she thought.

"Excellent. Now, Frances and Albert, join hands again and make your way slowly offstage."

Before Albert could put his death grip on her again, Frances lightly took his hand and half led, half pushed him offstage.

"Geeze," Albert muttered. There were little beads of sweat forming around his forehead.

Miss Leticia spent the rest of the lesson changing

roles. Frances got to be the rabbit and later a squirrel. She enjoyed every bit of it and was only sorry that Polly wasn't there to be part of this as well. Then it suddenly struck her that Polly would hate waltzing around the stage as much as Albert did.

After class all the girls were laughing about Albert.

"Did you see the way he clomped Terry on the head when she was Rabbit?" Tammi said, laughing.

"It hurt," Terry said, but she laughed too.

"I wonder when Albert's going to show up in tights?" someone else said. "After all, that's what real male ballet dancers wear, not gym shorts."

"Albert in tights!" Sheila shrieked. "I can't wait."

Frances couldn't wait either. He might have told the guys he was taking ballet lessons, but he certainly wouldn't let them know he was doing it in tights. She hoped he was looking through the curtain at this moment.

Frances left the dance studio with the other girls, but she hadn't gone a block when she realized she had left her book bag in the changing room. Hurrying back, she ran into Albert, who was just leaving.

"Well, that's it for me," he said importantly.

"What do you mean?"

"I just quit ballet."

"You're kidding," Frances said, taken aback. "What about your bicycle?"

"I don't need a bike that much. I don't need *anything* that much. I told Aunt Leticia to find herself some other sucker. And I'm going to tell my mom the same thing."

Frances doubted if he had handed in his resignation in quite that manner, but crossing her fingers, all she said was, "So you won't be coming back at all?"

"Don't look so happy about it."

But Frances was happy. She bounced into the changing room, found her book bag, and whistled a little tune as she left the studio again, even though her whistling left something to be desired.

As she walked home, Frances went over the whole afternoon in her mind. She had gotten up in front of the class—with Albert Bell at her side, no less—and it hadn't been that bad. It had been good, in fact. Despite the cold air, Frances could feel herself growing warm inside. She had done all that without Polly being next to her.

The first thing Frances did when she got home was call Polly. "Hi," she said happily.

"How did it go?" Polly asked nervously.

"Swell. Let me tell you all about it."

"Sounds like you had fun."

"I did. And I've got some other news."

"Yeah?"

Frances smiled. "I'm quitting the basketball team."

frances checked the mailbox on her way into the house after school on Friday. She knew that her mother brought in the mail every day, but she thought it didn't hurt to look again.

The box was empty, so Frances hurried into the house to see if there was any mail waiting on the hall table. There was, but none of it was for her.

With a sigh Frances went into the kitchen, where Grammy was, having a cup of tea and reading the newspaper. "How are you?" Frances said, rubbing her cheek against her grandmother's.

"How are you?" Grammy asked shrewdly as Frances took off her coat. "You don't look very happy."

"I don't know why Mr. Brock hasn't answered me yet," Frances burst out.

"It hasn't been that long, Frances."

"But I even gave him a phone number."

Grammy sipped her tea slowly. "He could be out of town, hon. And you have to consider the possibility that he might not answer at all."

"That would be mean," Frances said.

"We don't know Mr. Brock's reasons. Let's look on the bright side, though. You may hear from him yet."

"The pageant's on Sunday."

"So there's a couple of days for him to get in touch. Don't worry about it, Frances."

Talking to her grandmother always made Frances feel better. Taking a cookie from the plate on the table, she asked, "How long are you going to be staying, Grammy?"

"My cast comes off next week. I suppose I can go home any time after that."

"I wish you would stay longer."

Grammy laughed. "Mike probably wishes I would hurry up and get well so he could have his room back." Grammy couldn't make it up and down the steep basement stairs, so she had swapped rooms with Mike.

"Mike likes having you here, too," Frances argued. "Besides, he doesn't mind sleeping in the basement guest room. Nobody bothers him down there."

"Well, I'm anxious to get back to my own house, hon." Grammy patted Frances's hand. "But I've certainly liked being here with you."

Frances went upstairs to do her homework. Thinking about her grandmother made Frances even more sorry that Mr. Brock was not coming to the pageant. Frances knew she was lucky to have such a good family. Even Mike and Elizabeth, who could be pains, were still fun most of the time. All Polly had in Lake Lister was her mom.

Throwing herself on her bed, Frances wondered if she should have copied down Mr. Brock's phone number as well. Then she could call him. Staring up at the ceiling, she wondered if she would actually have the nerve to do that. She was getting braver, but she didn't think she was quite that brave yet.

"Frances, get up." Elizabeth was standing over her sister's bed, frowning.

Frances squinted at her sister. "What time is it?"

"Almost eight."

Frances rolled over. "Wake me at nine."

"No. Today's the dress rehearsal for the pageant. We've got to get going, Frances."

Now Frances sat up. How could she forget? Each room had been assigned a time to show up at the school. Frances's class was scheduled at nine, Elizabeth's at nine thirty.

"I'll take a shower and be downstairs in a flash," Frances said, rolling out of bed.

"Well, hurry." Elizabeth's voice sounded odd.

Frances stared at her sister. "What's wrong with your voice?"

"My voice?" Elizabeth croaked.

"Yes. Do you have laryngitis?"

"Don't be silly," Elizabeth said, but the words trailed off. "Maybe I do have a little cold. But I'll be fine."

"I hope so," Frances said with concern. She had teased Elizabeth about singing too much and losing her voice, but she certainly hoped that wasn't happening.

After a quick breakfast, Mr. McAllister drove the girls over to the school. "Do you need a ride back?" he asked when he dropped them off.

"Polly, Lena, and I don't. We're going to do some Christmas shopping."

"Downtown?" Elizabeth asked, making a face. "You have to go out to the mall to get anything really good."

"I don't want to hear that kind of talk," Mr. McAllister said sharply. Both girls looked at him in amazement. Mr. McAllister almost never raised his voice. A little more softly he said, "You know things are tough on Main Street. It doesn't help if my own family is negative about shopping there."

Even though Frances was coming out looking good in this situation, she felt bad for Elizabeth. Who knew their dad would be so upset about talk of the mall?

"Well, maybe I'll go downtown and look around too," Elizabeth said, trying to make amends.

Mr. McAllister patted her hand. "I know you will. Sorry I got so upset with you."

"Boy," Elizabeth said as they walked toward the school, "business at the store must be really bad."

"I heard Mom telling Grammy something about that in the kitchen, but when I walked in they stopped talking."

Elizabeth saw the worried look on Frances's face. "Hey, it'll be all right, Frances. There's been times when business hasn't been so hot, and we got through it."

Frances appreciated Elizabeth's efforts to buck her up. But she couldn't help noticing that her sister's voice was getting hoarser with each sentence she spoke. Now she had something else to worry about. Was Elizabeth going to be well enough to perform her solo?

The scene in the auditorium when the girls entered was a madhouse. Even though each class had an assigned time to practice, there were plenty of other people—adults and children—running around. Mothers were fitting kids for costumes, seventh and eighth graders from the junior high school were working on scenery, and off in a corner four horn soloists were tooting something that sounded vaguely like "We Wish You a Merry Christmas."

Mr. Winnow, looking harried, was waving the kindergartners dressed as Santa's elves off the stage. "All right," he bellowed, "my class, get ready to practice."

From various parts of the audience, Mr. Winnow's fourth graders gathered at the foot of the stage. Polly and Lena appeared from behind the curtain where they had been waiting while the little kids did their bit.

Mr. Winnow began taking attendance. "We're all here. Now let's get into our costumes. Then meet back here in ten minutes. Ten minutes on the dot." The boys and girls headed off to change, while Mr. Winnow slumped into one of the auditorium chairs.

"And it's only nine o'clock," Lena said, looking back at Mr. Winnow over her shoulder.

Polly followed her gaze. "I wonder if he's going to last until this afternoon."

"He does look frazzled."

But the dress rehearsal went pretty well. Albert Bell and Polly kept trying to outdo each other, which made for some funny moments. In the last scene, however, Polly pulled a little trick on Albert. It was the moment where Polly, as the real Santa, was supposed to invite Albert, the fake one, to come along and help deliver the presents. Polly should have handed Albert some gifts and said her line: "Won't you join me?"

Instead she handed him a canister with a decorated top and said, "Here's a present for you."

Unsuspecting, Albert opened it up and a huge rubber snake popped out.

Everyone onstage and in the auditorium started laughing, except Albert—and Mr. Winnow.

"Polly! What's the big idea?"

Polly tried to hide a grin. "Sorry, it was just a joke."

"It wasn't funny," Mr. Winnow snapped. "If you try anything like that during the actual performance . . ."

"I won't," Polly said, sounding contrite, but Frances could see her biting her lip, trying not to smile.

"You better not!"

Albert, still holding the empty canister in his hand, hissed, "I'm going to get you. Just wait."

"Aren't you worried?" Frances asked Polly after the rehearsal was over.

"Nah. He wouldn't dare do anything during the show."

"How did you have the nerve to do that?" Lena asked.

"I found that can while I was looking around my basement last night for something else. I knew Mr. Winnow wouldn't really do anything to me. Not the day before the performance."

Frances thought Polly had taken a big chance, but then that was Polly. She'd go a pretty long way for a joke.

The girls were putting on their coats, getting ready to go shopping, when the sixth grade began their skit. Elizabeth's solo came first. Frances stopped to listen. Then she wished she hadn't.

Elizabeth didn't sound very good. Although she was trying very hard, and her singing was right on key, the huskiness in her voice was even worse than it had been earlier. Frances could see how hard her sister was straining to hit the higher notes. She didn't want to hear any more. Turning away, Frances said to her friends, "Let's go shopping." But she was very upset. How was Elizabeth going to do her solo tomorrow?

Shopping on Main Street turned out to be more successful than Frances thought. She was able to buy a cookbook for her mother at the Book Nook and a little porcelain vase for Grammy at one of the antique shops that reopened for Christmas. Since her father always wanted the same thing for Christmas, Frances was able to pick up socks for him at Crawford's.

Polly and Lena weren't quite as lucky. "Maybe I should go over to your dad's hardware store and buy my mother a snow shovel," Polly joked. "She keeps talking about cleaning off the driveway."

Since it was almost lunchtime, the girls decided to go to the Sweet Shoppe for hamburgers. As they waited for their orders to come, the girls discussed every aspect of the show—who was good, who was bad, which classes had concocted interesting offerings, and which were bores. Finally Lena said, "Polly, are you sure you're not worried about pulling that trick on Albert?"

"Why?" Polly grinned. "You think he'll try to get back at me?"

"He might."

"Nah. I told you a million times. He'd never do anything the night of the show."

Frances hoped that Polly was right. But she had known Albert a lot longer than Polly had.

Elizabeth stood in the middle of the bathroom, tears rolling down her cheeks. "I can't do it," she croaked.

Frances and Elizabeth were supposed to be in the auditorium for the pageant in a half hour. All day Grammy had made tea with lemon and honey for Elizabeth to drink, hoping that would help her voice, but she was just as hoarse as ever. It was clear that Elizabeth couldn't go on.

The McAllisters' bathroom was small, but practically the whole family was crowded in there trying to make Elizabeth feel better.

"Aw, you'll get another chance," Mike said, awkwardly patting his sister's shoulder.

"Come on, now," Mr. McAllister said. "Let's get over to the school so you can talk to Mr. Winnow."

Mrs. McAllister ran cold water over a washcloth, wrung it out, and handed it to Elizabeth. "Here, sweetheart, put this over your eyes for a minute. You'll feel better."

Frances went into the bedroom with her sister. "I'm sorry, Elizabeth," she said quietly.

Elizabeth just nodded as she put on a sweater. Frances had never seen her sister look sadder.

The girls arrived at the auditorium early, but Mr. Winnow was already there, looking through some scripts.

"Do you want me to talk?" Frances whispered as they approached him.

"No, I will."

Mr. Winnow looked up. "Oh, hi, girls. I'm glad you're here early. I don't want to worry that people are coming in late."

Elizabeth cleared her throat. "Mr. Winnow," she began, barely audible. "I have a sore throat."

For a moment Mr. Winnow looked as if he didn't understand. Then a weary expression crossed his face. "You can't sing."

"She can hardly talk," Frances said.

Elizabeth's eyes filled with tears again, and now Mr. Winnow sprang into action. Grasping Elizabeth's hand in his, he said, "I know this must be a big disappointment for you, Elizabeth, but it's not the end of the world. We'll find someone to replace you. You would have done a wonderful job, but it's more important for you to rest your voice so you can get better and enjoy your Christmas vacation."

For the first time all day Elizabeth smiled.

"Now, I don't want you to worry about a thing. Maybe if you're not feeling too bad, you can assist me. I'll probably have lots of last-minute errands to run."

"I'd like to," Elizabeth murmured.

Frances heaved a sigh of relief. It was a good thing that Elizabeth had a crush on Mr. Winnow after all.

She would never have been this happy if Mrs. Graham, her own teacher and a woman of fifty with gray hair, had asked her to run errands.

Elizabeth may have been happy, but Mr. Winnow sighed. "Now, I wonder just who we can get to replace you?"

Suddenly Frances had an idea. "What about Lena Kroll? She has a beautiful voice."

Mr. Winnow perked up. "She does?"

"Oh, yes," Frances assured him.

"But she has quite a big part in our skit. And Elizabeth's class comes right after ours. She'd never have time to make the change." Mr. Winnow continued thinking out loud. "I can't change the order of the act now. It would just confuse everything."

"Well, there might be someone in another class," Frances suggested.

"But who? If only there was someone who could take Lena's role in the skit."

Frances felt her face redden. She knew Lena's part— she knew almost everyone's part—from going over Polly's lines with her. But if she told Mr. Winnow, he'd want her to get out on the stage and act.

Elizabeth glanced at Frances. She had heard Polly and Frances rehearsing, so she, too, knew that Frances could do the part of Mrs. Claus.

"Well, I'll think of something." Mr. Winnow sighed.

There were a few seconds of silence, then Frances cleared her throat. "I . . . uh, I could do Lena's part."

"You!" Mr. Winnow exclaimed.

Frances explained about working with Polly.

"Why didn't you say so?"

When Frances didn't answer right away, Elizabeth said, "She's a little shy.

Frances cringed. On the other hand, she was glad that Elizabeth had offered her a way out.

Mr. Winnow looked seriously at Frances. "I see. I should have guessed, considering how quiet Frances can be in class. I don't want to push you into anything, Frances. Do you think you could do it? Do you want to?"

Frances thought. A few months ago she would have said, never in a million years. Now she thought back to her last ballet class. She hadn't minded getting up in front of the group. Of course, that wasn't the same as getting up in front of an auditorium full of people. Feeling her stomach tighten, Frances said, "I don't think so."

"We'll make other arrangements then. It's all right, Frances," Mr. Winnow said.

But how could they make other arrangements, she thought. No one else knew Lena's lines. Mr. Winnow could probably get someone to do Elizabeth's solo and leave Lena as Mrs. Claus, but then Lena wouldn't have her chance to get up in front of the school and show them how well she could sing. That didn't seem fair, either.

If she really wanted to be a dancer, someday she was going to have to perform in front of an audience. Maybe she should start now. "Mr. Winnow, I've changed my mind. I'll do Lena's part."

"Are you sure, Frances?"

"I'm sure."

11

the next half hour was hectic. So hectic, Frances barely had time to get nervous. Lena arrived and was informed about the change in plans. She squealed with delight. "I'm really going to get to sing? I can't believe it."

Seeing the look on Lena's face made Frances happy she had decided to take her place. "You don't mind about not being Mrs. Claus?"

"Oh, no. I'd much rather sing."

When Polly arrived, however, and heard about the switch, she was in shock. "You're going to be Mrs. Claus? You're really going to get up in front of all those people?"

Frances could feel elephants starting to roam around in her stomach. "It's really not that big a part. I think I can do it."

Polly saw Frances's distress and quickly changed her tone. "Sure you can." Throwing her arm around Frances's shoulder, she asked, "Do you realize for a few minutes we're going to be husband and wife?"

That made Frances laugh, and the elephants lumbered away. At least for a little while. "You're not nervous at all, are you?" she asked Polly.

"Well, I might be, if my father was in the audience. . . ." Polly's smile faded.

Frances hadn't heard one word from Polly's father. Now she was very glad that she hadn't raised her friend's hopes by telling her about the letter. "There will be other times," she said softly.

"Sure." Polly brightened. "Maybe he'll see me at one of my basketball games."

I hope so, Frances thought.

Then it was time for everyone to get into costume. Frances had to hike up the skirt that Lena was supposed to wear, but other than that, with her wig and makeup, she was pleased with the way she looked. She could hear the audience filing in, but she tried not to think about that.

The kindergartners were just starting their song when a panicked Polly, dressed in her Santa outfit, came running over to Frances. "I can't find my beard," she said anxiously.

"Did you bring it from home?"

"Of course. It was in a brown paper bag. I put it down for a minute, but now it's gone."

"Where did you leave it?"

"Over there, by Mr. Winnow's desk." The girls were dressing in their classroom. The boys were next door in the library.

"Have you asked anybody if they've seen it?"

"No. I've just been looking for it."

"Well, let's ask."

Quickly they ran around questioning the other girls. When they asked Tammi, she said, "I thought I saw Albert with it."

"Albert!" Polly cried.

"I looked up and he was in here," Tammi said. "I thought he was trying to get a look at us while we were changing, even though no one was really undressed. I told him to get lost."

"And he had the bag?" Polly said.

Tammi wrinkled her brow. "I think so."

"Let's go," Polly said determinedly.

Frances ran after Polly, who was storming into the library. "Albert Bell," she bellowed, "where's my beard?"

"Your beard?" Albert tried to look innocent.

"Yes. I know you've got it."

"Prove it."

Polly had drawn a crowd with her accusation. "If you don't give me that beard, I'm going to tell Mr. Winnow."

Albert held out his arms. "Search me."

"I'll murder you!"

"You're going to ruin the skit," Frances said desperately.

Some of the girls had filtered into the library. Now they had gathered into a big circle along with the boys.

"Do you have that beard, Bell?" a boy named Tom asked.

Albert looked a little worried. "Why blame me?"

"Come on, Albert, give it back," Sheila said.

"You're going to ruin the play," Tammi told him angrily.

Susie the stage manager rushed in. "Get out there. You guys are on in about one minute."

"I can't go on without my beard," Polly wailed.

"Bell . . ." one of the bigger boys said threateningly.

"Aw, all right, keep your pants on." Albert hurried behind the librarian's desk and brought out the bag.

Polly snatched it away from him and put on the beard. "What a dumb trick," she said as she followed the rest of the class out to the stage.

"Almost as dumb as that stupid snake in a can."

"That was funny."

"Quiet, you two!" Susie hissed. "Get out there."

Frances had been so caught up in the drama of the missing beard, she hadn't had time to really get frightened. Now, with the stage lights blinding her a little, she could barely see the audience. It was easy to pretend she was out there all by herself. Before she knew it, Polly was speaking her opening line and Frances was answering her.

The whole skit passed like a dream. She had practiced the lines with Polly so much that she didn't have any trouble remembering them. In the last scene of the skit Mrs. Claus was supposed to do a little waltz with Santa. Frances smiled when it came time to do that part. She had dreamed about dancing onstage, but she had never pictured it happening like this.

Then it was over. The audience was applauding, and the cast was stepping out to take their bows. Now Frances could see the audience clearly, and the elephants came rushing back to her stomach. Before they could start tromping around, though, the curtain came down and the fourth graders left the stage.

Mr. Winnow's class was supposed to wait quietly in the library until the whole pageant was over, but Frances and Polly lingered in the wings long enough to hear Lena start her song. It was pure and clear and lovely.

Frances felt sorry for Elizabeth, but she was glad that Lena was giving such a wonderful performance.

The girls sneaked back into the library, and the first thing Polly did was look around for Albert. "Where is he?" she whispered. "I'm not done with him."

But Frances nudged her and pointed to the librarian, who had been recruited to maintain order. "Don't start anything now."

Albert, however, was nowhere to be seen. He had been very good in the skit—even Frances had to admit that. The role of the fake Santa was a funny one, and Albert had milked every bit of humor out of it.

"I guess he's scared to show his face," Polly muttered. She went off to go over the success of the skit with Tammi and some of the other kids.

Frances was ready to join her when she noticed Albert talking with a man out in the hall. There was something familiar about him, but Frances was sure she didn't know him. He was tall and on the broad side, and his hair was dark and wiry. She watched as Albert brought him into the room.

"Hey, Brock," he called. "Your father's here."

Frances watched with her mouth open as Polly ran across the library and threw herself into her father's arms.

"Hi, sweetie," he said with a smile.

"What are you doing here?" Polly demanded.

Frances held her breath. She hoped Mr. Brock wouldn't tell Polly she had written him. Polly would be much happier if she thought her dad had just come on his own.

Standing behind Polly, where only Mr. Brock could see her, Frances shook her head *no!*

For a moment Mr. Brock looked confused.

"I thought you had business you had to take care of," Polly said insistently.

Mr. Brock's face cleared. "I do. I have to leave in a few minutes, but I decided I could postpone my trip just long enough to see my daughter the star."

"Oh, Daddy." Polly buried her face in her father's shoulder.

Mr. Brock winked at Frances.

Polly pulled away. "There's somebody I want you to meet." She turned around and saw Frances. "Here she is. Daddy, this is my best friend Frances McAllister."

Mr. Brock put out his hand. "Very nice to meet you, Frances."

Shyly Frances took it. "Nice to meet you."

"You know, Polly, good friends are one of the most important things you can have."

"I know."

"I think Frances looks like a very good friend."

"Well, of course she is." Polly smiled at Frances. "The best."

Frances smiled back. It was nice to have a best friend again.

ILENE COOPER has written several children's books including the acclaimed *Kids from Kennedy Middle School* series. She has also written for television and is currently the children's book editor at *Booklist* magazine. When she's not reading or writing, she's knitting or traveling in England, her favorite country. She lives in Highland Park, Illinois, with her husband, a television director.

Wanted: One best friend

Frances in the Fourth Grade

FRANCES TAKES A CHANCE

by Ilene Cooper

Frances McAllister has always been shy, but she's always had her best friend, Bonnie, there to help her out. Now that Bonnie has moved away and practically ruined her life, Frances isn't sure how she's going to survive. Then she meets Polly Brock. Polly's new in town, and she wants to be Frances's friend. The only problem is Polly's a little overwhelming. Could Frances's first real friend in the fourth grade be more than she can handle?

FIRST TIME IN PRINT!

A BULLSEYE BOOK PUBLISHED BY ALFRED A. KNOPF, INC.